BECOMING
BEATRIZ

BECOMING
BEATRIZ

TAMi CHARLES

Charlesbridge
TEEN

Published by Charlesbridge
85 Main Street
Watertown, MA 02472
(617) 926-0329
www.charlesbridgeteen.com

Library of Congress Cataloging-in-Publication Data
Names: Charles, Tami, author.
Title: Becoming Beatriz / by Tami Charles.
Description: Watertown, MA : Charlesbridge, [2019] | Companion to: Like
    Vanessa. | Summary: "In 1984 Newark, Beatriz Mendez navigates romance,
    gang culture, and her family's past. After her gang-leader brother is killed,
    Beatriz gives up her dreams of dancing in order to run the gang. But her
    eyes are reopened to her dream of a career in dance when the school brainiac
    asks her to compete in a dance competition with him—but will the gang let
    her go?"—Provided by publisher.
Identifiers: LCCN 2018031378 (print) | LCCN 2018046987 (ebook) |
    ISBN 9781632896117 (ebook) | ISBN 9781580897785 (reinforced for library use)
Subjects: LCSH: Puerto Ricans—New Jersey—Newark—Juvenile fiction. |
    Haitian Americans—Juvenile fiction. | Hispanic American gangs—New
    Jersey—Newark—Juvenile fiction. | Female gang members—Juvenile fiction.
    | Teenagers—Juvenile fiction. | Dance—Juvenile fiction. | Ethnic relations
    —Juvenile fiction. | Nineteen eighties—Juvenile fiction. | Newark (N.J.)—
    History—20th century—Juvenile fiction. | CYAC: Puerto Ricans—New
    Jersey—Newark—Fiction. | Haitian Americans—Fiction. | Gangs—
    Fiction. | Dance—Fiction. | Ethnic relations—Fiction. | Newark (N.J.)—
    History—20th century—Fiction.
Classification: LCC PZ7.1.C4915 (ebook) | LCC PZ7.1.C4915 Be 2019 (print)
    | DDC 813.6 [Fic]—dc23
LC record available at https://lccn.loc.gov/2018031378

Printed in the United States of America
(hc) 10 9 8 7 6 5 4 3 2 1

Display type set in GFY Woodward and Coffeedance by the Chank Company
Text type set in Adobe Caslon Pro by Adobe Systems Incorporated
Printed by Berryville Graphics in Berryville, Virginia, USA
Production supervision by Brian G. Walker
Designed by Joyce White

DEAREST NASSER,
YOU REALLY DO LOOK LIKE THE REST OF MY LIFE.

BESOS,
TAMI

ACT 1: UNRAVELING

¡FAMA!
QUIERO VIVIR
PA' SIEMPRE.

—BEATRIZ, AGE 12, 1981
(FIRST GRAFFITI TAG AS A DIABLA)

FRIDAY, APRIL THIRTEENTH

THEY SAY WHEN YOU see a wishmaker flower, you're supposed to make a wish and blow.

I thrust my body to the ground, press my face to the pavement, and wish away the first gunshot and the panicked faces and screaming voices circling around my 'hood. The wishmaker juts out of a gap in the sidewalk—pays me no attention. Instead it searches the sky for the sun and leaves me realizing this shit's all my fault. I should've let Junito be.

Crack! The second shot rings out louder than the first. I still hear the radio from the bodega blasting Héctor Lavoe and Willie Colón's "Todo tiene su final." A minute ago, I'd begged Junito to dance salsa with me. Ignored his warnings to stay in the house today. Pulled him into the rhythm and lost myself in the lyrics—everything has an end.

Ain't this some bull.

Crack! Crack! More bullets soar above us, shattering the window of our bodega. Shards of glass land on me. I pant through heavy breath and squinted eyes, screaming my brother's name. I turn my head and see Junito reach for the Glock in his boot. He aims it at the silver Trans Am and pops off a couple rounds.

It's not cold out, but I shiver. Questions fill me up faster than bullets slice the air. Who ordered this hit? Why does God hate me? Because that's the only explanation I got for him making my birthdate and death date one in the same.

And who made up that stupid wishmaker flower saying anyway? Because whoever did can kiss my nalgas. Twice.

The silver Trans Am comes to a screeching halt in front of the bodega.

More shots.

Who are they? What do they want?

Junito jolts upright, glass falling off of him, and fires off again. I stay on the ground, my chest heaving in and out, tiny pieces of asphalt piercing my cheek.

But then tires skid and smoke against the asphalt before accelerating down Broadway. Just like it happens in the movies. This is the magic of Junito Mendez. No matter what, he always forces the bad guys away. I'd seen it before—but not like this, not this bad, not this close to home.

DQ yells out from the bodega, "We're good in here!"

"Todo bien!" Mami cries out, but I can hear the lie in her voice. On the surface, we're fine. Just a busted store window and some penny-candy buckets with fresh bullet holes. Look a little deeper, though, and you'd see the truth.

Junito stands up and flashes DQ a knowing look. Then he starts to run down the alley toward the empty lots. And even though he told me to stay inside earlier, I follow him. Listening is not my thing apparently. The farther I run, the quieter the music gets.

"Don't worry. They're gone." I can barely get the words out from trying to keep up.

Junito whips his head around fast, the anger in his eyes stabbing right through me.

"What are you doing? I told you to stay back!" His voice is untamed.

"Why didn't *you* stay?" My voice matches his now.

We finally stop running and tuck ourselves against the brick wall of the abandoned alley, positioned between two buildings.

"I don't need to be on the scene when the police show up, that's why. Por dios, you don't listen!" Junito pulls two loose bricks from the bottom of the wall, wipes the Glock clean, and tries to hide it in the empty space. He can't make it fit.

In the distance, I hear the faint sound of sirens, see Junito frantically searching his pockets.

"¡Carajo!" he curses.

"Why were they coming for you, Junito? Tell me right now!" I demand.

In the past, we've had one, maybe two gangs outside of Newark try to claim our spot. Never worked though. Junito was a force like that. Either you bowed down or you caught the heat.

Junito finds the switchblade in his boot and starts pounding out another brick like mad. "Not today, Beatriz. All you gotta know is I ain't letting nobody take over what I built. And sometimes you gotta send a message to let people know that."

Translation: Something went down last night and Junito started a war.

"Oh yeah? And if these pendejos don't back down like the others? What then?" My voice loses its balance.

Junito finally gets the brick loose and jams the gun inside. "You ain't gotta worry about that."

He wraps his arm around my shoulder and pulls me in real slow. Together, we take turns breathing. Inhala, exhala. Just like Mami always says to calm us down.

"Let's wait a couple more minutes before we go back, and when five-o starts asking questions, let me do the talking," Junito says. "Everything will be fine."

I want to believe Junito. That it'll be okay.

"Let's talk about something else," Junito insists.

I lift my face to the midmorning sky, picture myself flying through those clouds. "You ever wonder what you could be outside of this place?"

Junito fixes his eyes real hard on the ground. I know this ain't no kind of life for us. He knows it too. But what choice do we have? Go back to being dirt poor, like we were when we first got here? Or worse, return to Aguadilla? Even if I wanted us to go back to the island, I already know what his answer would be. *Hell no. There's a monster waiting for us there.*

"I'd start fresh . . . in San Francisco." Junito hesitates before he says the last part.

I feel a sharp twinge in my stomach. Because deep down I know who he would go there for. The infamous TJ Martin.

"Anyway, that ain't possible right now." Junito adds the switchblade to the hole and slips the first brick in.

A familiar voice creeps inside my head. The one that repeats over and over again that I'm the reason Junito can't live the way he wants. But I won't carry that load all by myself. Papi's the first to blame. Then me. And the Diablos.

I look at my watch. The tick of each second feels like an eternity. I'd spent the morning practicing the dance for my quinceañera and then dodging bullets. Tonight I would have to pretend that none of this ever happened.

"There's gonna come a day when we won't have to do this no more, Junito. One day I'll be a professional dancer and make enough money to buy Mami one of those big houses over in Vailsburg or Mount Vernon. Maybe even away from Jersey." I face him square on.

But Junito laughs, pointing the second brick my way. "What I tell you about watching that stupid show *Fame*? That's television, pipe-dream stuff. This is reality."

Anger builds up inside. "Whatever, Junito!"

"When you live in a city where cocaine is king, dancing ain't gonna pay the bills." He crawls to the edge of the building and takes a peek down the alley.

Junito doesn't know what he's talking about. Right there in the midst of the abandoned buildings tagged with my first graffiti—*Fame, I'm gonna live forever*—in the empty field where my dancing dreams once bloomed, I envision a life far away from this place.

I don't notice there's someone behind me. Only hear the click of a gun and feel the hot metal kissing the back of my head.

"Looks like we get a two-for-one today." His accent sounds like he's from Nigeria or something, mixed with French too.

I suck in air, turn around, and see a yellow-scarfed face and two eyes burning like a distant sun.

Junito springs up. His legs take flight, arms like wings, he throws the brick in his hand at homeboy, knocking the gun out of his hand. The sickening sounds of cracked noses and hard blows to the gut ring over and over. Junito bobs to the right, the dude weaves to the left. And there I sit, staring at the dude's gun a few feet away from me and Junito's neatly tucked in the wall. Hypnotized by the sounds and the fiery eyes in them both, an inner voice cries out: *Get the hell up, Beatriz. Grab a gun. Any gun.*

My wrist turns limp as I dig into the hole, wrap my fingers around the trigger, and rise up to finish him off.

Before I can do anything, homeboy gives me a swift punch to my right cheek, the gun tumbling out of my hand. The crunch of my jawbone is like a bomb going off inside of me. The whole universe spins, and I pull out the blade I keep hidden inside my left cheek.

Homeboy comes in for the double hit, his fist like heavy metal against my face.

My hand slips, and the blade slices through the guy's bandana not even a full inch. He screams as the bandana falls to the ground, revealing a thick goatee and a holy cross symbol tattooed on his neck. A single red drop of blood dances through his beard and lands on his shirt.

"Oh, you messed up now," he says, grasping a chunk of my hair in his oversized hands. Junito flies in for an uppercut, but instead catches a foot to the gut that sends him airborne. I punch and punch at the air, at this messed-up life, and at homeboy until I'm out of breath. But he just lifts me from the ground and throws me headfirst against the Dumpster. My back arches in slow motion until it crashes against the asphalt. I lie there, unmoving.

He stomps his foot against my jaw again, and my whole world goes black.

Behind closed eyes, I can hear the sound of my heartbeat pulsing through my head, feel the release of his foot. Hear the pounding, blow by blow, as Junito continues the fight.

He'll get to his gun, or even homeboy's, and finish the job. Three years as a Diabla and my body count is still zero. I've never even touched a gun until now. The small blade hidden in my mouth has always been my only weapon. And Junito wants to keep it that way.

Any second now and this will be all over. Junito and I will run home and put on the biggest show for the police.

Officer: Where were you during the drive-by, young man?

Junito: Officer, my sister and I were taking a stroll in the neighborhood. We weren't even here.

I'll get ready for my quinceañera, because turning fifteen is a big deal. Go with Mami to pick up Abuela from the airport. Let them both have their way with me. Do my hair, fluff my dress, all that proper "señorita" nonsense. That'll make Mami happy. I mean, the woman sold her other bodegas to pull off this expensive-behind, wannabe wedding.

A single shot rings out. The blast courses through my entire body, seems to echo all throughout Grafton and Broadway like an explosion thundering in the sky. I can't move. It's like someone presses pause on the entire city of Newark. The music, the sirens, the cars—they all disappear.

But when the darkness of my mind clears, and I open

my eyes, it's Junito who I see lying on the ground, shaking uncontrollably, hands pressed against his chest—blood erupting like a busted fire hydrant in the dead of July. I beg my legs to move, to get up and push me toward Junito, but homeboy's not done with me. He locks his rock-hard boot on my shoulder, points the gun at the space between my eyes. I lie there helpless, thunder moving through me as I watch Junito bleed and bleed.

"This is for Gaston. Got that, muchacha?" He leans down into my face and the heat of his breath finds its way to my skin.

Confusion floods in, wild and unforgiving. *Who the hell is Gaston?*

"Just hurry up and get it over with." He's going to shoot me too. Keep my eyes on the clouds. God's up there, waiting for me. Even though I'm pissed at him right now. I count down the seconds until I see the white light: *Five . . . four . . . three . . .*

Before I can reach *two*, homeboy leans down again and puts his lips close enough to brush against my earlobe. Drops of his blood fall on my shoulder. He whispers: "Nou pap janm bliye."

What did he just say?

I hear a car and turn my head. At the end of the alley, the silver Trans Am screeches to a halt, and the passenger door flies open.

He releases his foothold, grabs his bandana off the ground, and runs away, with his gun in his right hand and Junito's in his left. When he gets to the car, he does the strangest thing. He turns around, flails his arms out like wings, takes a bow, and yells out, "You talk? We'll be back."

I lock eyes with the person driving the car. Study the image from a distance. It's a girl. Dark sunglasses cover her eyes. Mounds and mounds of blonde dreadlocks spill out from her bandana. Another yellow bandana covers her mouth. She pulls it down, puckers her fire-red lips, and blows a kiss. Homeboy hops in, and they speed off under a sun-filled sky.

My legs finally give me permission to move. I roll over, grab my stomach, and vomit what feels like everything I've ever eaten for the past fifteen years.

"Get up, Junito!" It hurts to say each word. I wipe the blood from my mouth with the sleeve of my shirt and run toward my brother.

"¡Ayúdenlo!" I scream, but my jaw is locking.

The sirens grow louder, closer. I press a hand hard on Junito's chest, begging him to hold on just a little longer.

"They're coming. I hear them." More pain fires up in my jaw.

"I'll . . . be . . . okay. Don't . . . leave . . . Diablos . . ." I cover his lips before he can finish his sentence.

"Diabla for life!" I'm sobbing now. "Te lo juro."

Junito stops shaking, and I scream, "Don't leave me!" over and over again. Out of nowhere, the cops come running down the alley, guns drawn, mouths moving in slow motion.

My ears become soundproof. All I see is them gesturing for me to lie on the ground. Like a dog. Hands behind my head. Feet together. Don't move. Be still. But I move uncontrollably. One cop jumps on top of me. Then another. I can't breathe. Half my face is pressed into the grass. I wonder if Junito's gone already. If he sees the white light, like I do, coming down from the sky. Then I feel more hands. Damn near fifty of them, exploring my body, searching for something, anything, to connect the dots. My lips position themselves to speak. One final crack in my jaw kills all of my words.

"We need to check the kid's pulse!" someone yells.

Yes, save him please! Hurry! I plead inside my head.

Someone tosses me on a gurney. Places two fingers on my wrist and starts counting. Slaps a mask on my face. Rolls me toward a flashing swirl of red, white, and blue. Doors shut. Engine roars. Tires screech. Last thing I see out the back window is Junito lying in the field like some kind of science project.

CONVERSATIONS WITH FIVE-O

"MY NAME IS DETECTIVE Osario and this is my partner, Detective Green. How are you feeling today?"

Como mierda, I curse in my head. What day is it? Where am I? All I see are white walls, white blinds, and Mami standing by a door too far for me to reach. There are two faces staring back at me, one in particular too close to my own. I close my eyes, wishing the moment away, but an image I'll never forget appears. Dark skin, sliced chin dripping with blood, yellow bandana curtseying its way to the asphalt. That crooked smile. And those words. . . . What were they again? New pop blay?

The memory sends electric bolts through every part of my body. The room tilts back and forth, side to side, until the dude's face and his words melt away, leaving behind Detective Osario speaking at a snail's pace.

"¿Cómo te sientes, Beatriz?"

What does this guy want from me? What's going on? I move my head frantically, searching for Junito, each twist of my neck sending panic through my body. My hands are covered in tubes connected to machines that beep, beep, beep.

Mami stands at the door, hands pressed against tear-stained cheeks, whispering "Cálmate, mi amor. Inhala, exhala."

The guy wants to know how I'm feeling? Certainly not calm, like Mami's telling me to be. Beat down to the ground. That's what I got going on inside. I start to say that until I realize that my teeth won't separate.

"It's okay," the other guy, Detective Green, says. "You're at Clara Maass Hospital. You sustained a pretty bad injury to your jaw, so the doctors had to wire your mouth shut."

"We waited a few days, but the doctors say you should be able to speak by now, even with your jaw wired," the first cop adds.

My breathing speeds up. I can feel my heart hitting my chest with a mean uppercut.

"Do you have any idea who did this to you . . . and your brother?" They're both talking now. One starts, the other finishes.

My lips are dry. So very dry. Any second, they are gonna crack. Fall off. And I'll become lipless. Lipless Beatriz.

"Where . . . is . . . Junito?" I don't recognize my own voice, muffled behind sealed teeth and ready-to-fall-off lips.

The detectives look at each other a moment too long, before Detective Osario grabs a chair and pulls it to the bed I'm trapped in. Pain stabs me in the jaw the second I inhale a little too deep.

"One thing at a time, Beatriz. Can you give us a description of the car or perhaps the assailant who attacked you?" he asks.

My eyes close. The silver Trans Am appears, the sound of bullets overpowering the music, the fire in that dude's eyes as he pounced on Junito, and then there was her. And the black smoke left behind as homegirl drove the car down the alley and up Broadway.

"Beatriz?"

My eyes fly open. I shake my head no, over and over again, until the pain causes a scream to explode from my gut. "I ain't seen nothing!" I yell.

But I'm pretty sure it sounds more like *gahhhhhhhhh!*

Mami comes running to my bedside.

"That's it! Now you heard her!" Each word crashes into the next. "Haven't we been through enough? If you don't mind, I need to go to the ICU and check on my son."

Wait. Junito's here? Get these tubes off of me! I want to see my brother!

My eyes start to roll backward. Just then I hear the sound of familiar footsteps. Loud, swishy, nerve-shattering. It's been years since I've heard them, but I remember like it was yesterday.

"Ahora no es un buen momento." That's my abuela. She's here and already kicking people out. Typical.

Everything is a blur. We were supposed to pick her up from the airport in the afternoon. But then . . . the music . . . and the shots . . . and the sirens.

"I understand, Señora Vento," Detective Osario says, "but we do have reason to believe that this shooting is gang related."

Abuela clutches her rosary. "No mi nietos, no, no. Son niños buenos."

My stomach churns at the thought of Abuela believing we are those same good kids skipping rope and singing songs back in Aguadilla.

"We'd like to gather information from Beatriz about Junito and his alleged gang involvement so we can prosecute whoever did this," Detective Green adds.

"My . . . son . . . is . . . not . . . some . . . gangbanger!" Mami raises her voice.

I just want to rip these tubes off of me. Hold Mami. Tell her I'm sorry. That Junito is too. And that this won't happen again because Junito will take care of everything. He always does.

Abuela steps to Detective Osario. She's so close, and he towers over all four foot eleven of her. "¿Y qué va pasar si vuelven? ¿Nos van a proteger?"

My grandmother, Liliana Vento, has always been the feistiest lady in Aguadilla. The one who not only talked with her mouth, but also with a chancleta in her hand. But here, in this moment, in front of these suited-up policemen, she turns into someone I don't recognize. These pendejos don't care about protecting us, nor about the other gang that put us up in here.

They just grab their things and walk past Abuela and that puppy-dog look on her face.

Detective Osario stops short at the door. "You know, Beatriz, someone is gonna go down for this. It's unfortunate that you didn't see anything."

It's hard to look tough when you're covered in hospital tubes. That don't stop me from trying though. I pucker

my lips, roll my eyes, and remember the code: *Never snitch.*
I saw nothing. Don't want to talk about one piece of that
day, especially homeboy's promise that he'd come back if I
opened my mouth. Thinking about it is hard enough. Especially those other words he whispered: new pop blay. Soon
as I bust outta this joint, I'll write them down. Junito and I
will find out what the hell they mean. 'Cause somebody put
a hit out on my brother and there ain't a damn thing those
cops can do about it. But me and Junito will.

As the detectives leave the room, more footsteps find
their way in. Three doctors. Arms folded. Lips sagging. Eyes
looking like they ain't slept in days.

"May we have a word with you privately, Mrs. Mendez?"

14 arrested, 1 charged with murder

NEWARK, New Jersey
By: Keesha Lester

On Friday, April 13, alleged leader of the Latin Diablos gang, Juan "Junito" Mendez, was gunned down behind his storefront apartment in the Grafton Projects area of Newark. He died of his injuries just two days later at Clara Maass Hospital. Police have announced Clemenceau "Soukie" Mondesir, of the Macoute gang, as their prime suspect in Mendez's murder. Police believe that Mondesir may have had an accomplice, though no further arrests have been made.

After surveilling the Macoutes' activity for several weeks, Newark police raided an abandoned warehouse in the South Ward. At the scene, thirteen additional members of the Macoutes were found with a collection of firearms, marijuana, and two kilograms of heroin, which holds a street value of $10 million. Further undisclosed evidence was discovered, linking Mondesir to the death of Mendez.

Essex County Sheriff David D'Alessio has confirmed an initial appearance in court scheduled for Monday, April 23. Two of the 14 people arrested, Clemenceau Mondesir included, are Elizabeth, New Jersey, residents and suppliers of narcotics. Police were unable to link Mendez to the drugs or the gang itself. The act of violence seems to have been unsolicited.

The Macoute gang appears to be a copycat of the Tonton Macoute, a military regime created by François Duvalier, former president of Haiti. Under Duvalier's control, the Tonton Macoute were notorious for violence, corruption, and human rights violations.

Authorities confirm that the local New Jersey gang is composed of young Haitian immigrants, operating mainly in Elizabeth, East Orange, and most recently, the South Ward of Newark.

During the initial appearance, the judge will announce the charges against the defendants: heroin and cocaine possession with intent to sell and distribute, which carries a sentence of up to 25 years, along with second degree felony possession of an unlicensed weapon, which carries a ten-year sentence. With an additional charge of murder, Mondesir also faces 25 to life.

Given the severity of the charges, it is likely that bail will be denied for all defendants. City police will continue to crack down on gang and drug activity.

FAST FORWARD:
SEPTEMBER THE FOURTH

I'VE GOTTEN REAL GOOD at communicating with Mami. It's her eyes that tell her story. Those dull, gray eyes used to be green. Funny how the color of sadness comes in different shades.

"You gonna miss me today?" I ask as I brush Mami's teeth for her.

She looks at me frantically, wordlessly, her spine curving into a deep C.

"Inhala, exhala, Mami."

Breathing deep, she settles on staring at the floor.

"School's starting back up. But don't worry, I'll be here as much as I can," I say to reassure her.

I run a hot bath for her and brush her salt-and-pepper hair. Once upon a time, Mami's hair was dark as midnight and so long it reached her elbows. Now the bristles of the brush pull all two inches of her hair straight, before it springs back to super-short curls again. Mami hacked it off not long after they lowered Junito into the ground. That was the last day she found a pair of scissors in the house. Abuela made sure of it.

I dry Mami off, put a clean bata on her—a yellow house dress with blue flowers. I slip into the kitchen, away from Mami's eyes. Place the tiny blade inside my cheek. *Protection, always.* Junito's voice swirls inside my head, as fresh as the day he taught me to carry the blade when I was twelve.

I stuff my pockets, bra, and backpack with nickel bags of reefer. Sweat builds on the palms of my hands. *Time to start thinking 'bout getting back in the game, princesa.* Such an easy thing to say when you're playing the hero. And that's what DQ's been doing, five months strong. Making runs, selling dope, holding meetings at his spot, while I block that day out, make peace that the Macoutes are in lockup, and wait for the storm to pass.

It never did.

DQ wasn't in the empty lots. He didn't see Junito's begging eyes. Didn't hear that dude's threat. That was all for me.

I return to the living room to help Mami walk down the stairs to the bodega. Each step down is slow, like she's not sure if she can make the next one. By the time we finally reach the first floor, Abuela yells, "¡Buenos días, Mirta!"

Mami doesn't acknowledge her.

Eyes fixed on the door, Mami grabs her milk crate and zombie-walks straight toward the exit. There she'll sit all day, eyes staring at the ground, the very last place she saw Junito standing. She hopes and prays for him to come back to her, I think.

My stomach starts rumbling louder than I care it to.

"Maybe I'll skip school today?" I say aloud to no one in particular.

The cashier, Ms. Geraldine, makes a low moaning sound, like she wants to give her two cents. She stays quiet, which is good because one nosy grandmother is about all I can handle.

"¡Escúchame, Beatriz!" Abuela screams from the back of the bodega. She continues in Spanish. "You're going and that's it. It's time to live again."

The door to the bodega flies open. My girls Julicza and Maricela diva-stroll in like they're ready to walk the runway.

"First day, nenas!" Maricela shouts her way through the candy aisle, while Julicza picks up a couple of boxes of Lemonheads and sticks them straight in her pocket without paying.

Some things never change.

"Yo, you want us to wait for you while you get ready?" Maricela smacks on a piece of gum.

"And, girl, when you gonna get a touch-up?" Julicza grabs a chunk of my hair. "I never seen you with roots this nappy."

Flames shoot up and down my body. My crew is looking fresh to death. Meanwhile I'm rocking baggy overalls, a wrinkled-up T-shirt, and hair that's begging me to hit it with a relaxer.

"I'll just roll in, set everybody up, and book it before first period," I say quietly so Ms. Geraldine and Abuela can't hear me.

Maricela scrunches up her face like I must be crazy, stepping up on the first day of school looking homeless.

Usually all three of us go shopping together in downtown Newark a few weeks before school starts. Every year, we'd come home stacked—fresh Adidas, Guess jeans, T-shirts, and bamboo earrings with our name in them, at least two pairs. All that and then some, courtesy of that good ole Diablo cash flow. For the past few months, though, the cops had a crackdown on the whole city. DQ kept the operation going, but made sure the Diablos kept a low profile. Like clockwork, DQ hit me off with a cut, even though I did nothing to deserve one cent. Left me to grieve the first few months. Told me to come back when I'm ready.

Today's the day.

"You look just *fine*, nena." Maricela couldn't lie straight if somebody paid her.

"Word." Julicza tries to make it seem true, but I know better.

I scan the floor, searching for a different excuse. Like Mami's got a doctor's appointment or something, which would just add to the pack of lies because everybody in the 'hood knows that Mirta Mendez lost her shit on Friday the thirteenth and is way beyond repair.

My hair swells around my face. Maricela pulls a chunk of it back and sticks it behind my ear. It refuses and pops back into place.

"Your face is starting to look like it used to," she says.

This time I want to believe her. But deep down I know I am the opposite of what I looked like when I was the flyest girl in eighth grade. Ever since homeboy bashed my cheek in, I stopped hoping the day would come where I'd look like my old self. So I let my hair grow thicker, longer than it's ever been before, in an effort to hide the ugliness that remains.

"Here, put these on." Julicza takes the gold bangles off her wrist. "They're only fourteen karat gold, but they'll do."

"Ooh, and how about this?" Maricela reaches in her backpack for a red bandana to pull half of my hair into a ponytail. The other half falls just where I need it to.

"There. Now you look fresh to death. I think we're ready to show Barringer High who's in charge!" Julicza squeals.

I muster up a weak smile.

"We saw your mami outside." Maricela grabs a grape soda and heads to Ms. Geraldine to actually pay for it.

"Did she say anything to you guys?" Hope swells in my chest for a split second.

"Nah. She didn't even look up at us when we talked to her."

And just like that, my spirit sinks. I swear I wanna stay home so bad, but then I hear Junito's voice in my head. *It's the first day of school. Showtime.*

After the big Macoutes drug bust, cops were all up in our face, looking for a reason to get us too. They never found a solid piece of evidence. DQ stepped up and handled that.

Abuela flicks on the radio, startling me out of my thoughts. The last thing I want to hear right now is music, especially salsa.

"Abuela, turn the radio off and just play your telenovelas," I tell her.

But with the music booming and the empanada fryer bubbling so loudly, she can barely hear me.

"¿Qué dices, Beatriz?" Abuela yells over the trumpet.

I storm to the mini-kitchen located behind the register. "I said no music, por favor. Watch your telenovelas. They're quieter, and you can keep an eye on Mami that way."

Abuela brushes her hand on my cheek, smiles, and then gives me two good whacks upside the head.

"¡Ay! What was that for?" I rub my head.

Abuela turns down the radio. "Uno pa' tu amiga. La cubana que nunca paga. Y otra porque tu la deja."

She's had enough of Julicza always "forgetting" to pay for her stuff, and me letting her get away with it.

"Vete a estudiar." Abuela shoos me off to school.

Outside DQ is glued to the wall of the bodega, eyes fixed on Mami. Paco and Fredito are already cornered up nearby, on Broadway at Grafton and Halleck.

"Yo, Beatriz, you know what to do today, right?" DQ asks, as though I've already forgotten. Three years deep in the gang and even though Junito's not here, I still remember everything he taught me. But to be sure, DQ and I met last night to go over the plan.

"Don't you worry," I tell him. "I'm ready."

The sky turns a little cloudy just as the 25 bus pulls up and the doors screech open.

Maricela and Julicza walk on ahead of me.

"Yo, Beatriz!" DQ calls out just as I place my foot on the first step. "You packin', right?"

I pat my left cheek to show him I'll be just fine. I still haven't stepped up to packing a Glock—Junito would've never approved anyway. For now, a blade tucked inside my cheek will be enough to use on anybody who tries to step. Doubt anyone will, though.

I give my student ticket to the bus driver. Maricela, Julicza, and I find some seats in the back of the bus. The ride to Barringer isn't that long, but it's definitely too far to walk. Next year when I turn sixteen, I'll be able to drive. I'll get a car—a Pontiac Sunbird, and anything older than 1984 won't do. Me and my girls will ride to school in style.

Someone is playing music in the front of the bus. Homeboy's got a boom box propped on his shoulder. "Jam on It" comes on, and the whole bus comes alive. Everybody's popping to the beat. Even the old abuela in the middle row is getting down.

"Come on, muchacha, you know this song is fly." Julicza grabs my hand and tries to get me to dance, but I don't budge.

"Aw, man, you used to go berserk on the dance floor, Beatriz. I miss that." Maricela starts doing the snake in her seat.

Key words: *used to.*

I used to feel rhythm in every move I made. But these days, I just beg for it to go away. To leave me alone. Because the last thing I remember is the music and dancing with my brother, followed by running and gunshots. So, no. There ain't gonna be no more dancing.

And no matter how fresh that beat is (because, ¡ay Dios mío!, it really is), it'll never bring Junito back.

We hop off the bus and start walking down Park Avenue toward Clifton Street. The Cathedral Basilica towers over the sea of students as we move toward the school.

Barringer High. Population: fifteen hundred students, eighty-four teachers, and six security guards.

Translation? A lot of potential customers.

The back of the school is located on a dead-end street, and the rest of it takes up at least three blocks. It's packed when we finally get there, and just as DQ schooled me, it's easy to figure out who's who. The freshmen are all huddled by the Barringer signs waaay down the block, like they're scared as hell to even look at any of the older kids. They're probably realizing that eighth grade is long behind them and that their big-dawg middle-school status is over. The sophomores are a little farther up, huddled by the blue auditorium doors, probably happy they're not the small fish in the big pond anymore.

The juniors and seniors are sort of together. Already looking like they're over it, and the bell ain't even ring yet.

Time to get busy.

I scan the crowd, looking for my runners. Junito made sure I knew who they all were last year when I was in eighth grade. The rules are always clear. Every grade needs a boy and a girl. They share the responsibility of making sure orders are taken and distributed. Me? Stay away from the product once it's transferred. Keep my nose and hands clean. Once the runners get the product, it's their job to sell it. All of it . . . or face the consequences. Fridays are meetings, held in an empty storage room beneath our bodega. Take attendance. Drop your load. Me and DQ take our cut. Divvy up the funds. Set up the next round of sales. Meeting adjourned.

Repeat.

Repeat.

David "Mooki" Sanchez is my top pick for the freshman class. He's been down with me since sixth grade.

Maricela was more than happy to volunteer to cover ninth grade with him. But I know that has more to do with getting David's attention than actually being of any help.

"What's up, Beatriz? Good to see you." David gives me the signature Diablo handshake, and I slip five nickel bags in his pocket. To some, it might look like I'm grabbing his junk. But me and him know the deal.

For the sophomore class, Nilda Perez and Juan Diaz keep their spots from last year. They notice me before I even see them. They walk over, give me a handshake, and the deal is done.

Two grades down. Two to go.

The junior class was supposed to have Victoriano Lopez and Damarys Novaro as the runners, but last year Victor took a hit for Junito and got locked up for the next four years. Never snitched. Never said a word about our operation. A real soldier. And Damarys got pregnant by Victor right before he went in. Every Diablo knows there's only three ways to get out of the gang: death, get a beatdown that leaves you barely able to walk, or, if you're a girl, get pregnant. Needless to say, I was gonna have to recruit two new runners for the junior class.

Tony Pedros is our top seller at Barringer. Has been since he first got here his freshman year. The thing about Tony is that if you look at him, you'd never know that he's a dealer. B-plus student. Captain of the football team. He's got this whole existence outside the Diablos. And because Junito always thought he had a chance to get drafted in the NFL, Tony's literally the only Diablo that got a pass— didn't have to put as much time in with the gang so he'd have room for sports.

Tony seeks me out in the crowd. Valerie Reyes follows behind him. She's keeping her spot alongside Tony as female runner this year for the senior class.

"Glad to see you're back in the game, princesa," Tony whispers in my ear as he hugs me close. He smells of soap and Airheads and hunger. But that hunger won't last for long. While I'm wrapped in his arms, I weasel my hand through my sweatshirt and up to my bra. Nice and smooth. No one even notices. I slip enough bags in his pocket for him to split with Valerie.

"How you feeling, girl?" Valerie asks, with real concern in her eyes.

I shrug my shoulders and look around at the crowd.

"I'm maintaining. Pero oye, no Junito talk. I'm good. Trust me." My words are a Band-Aid over a still-open wound.

Just as the bell rings, I can sense a pair of eyes hawking me from the direction of the auditorium doors. When I turn, I see some tall dude with dark brown skin and a curly black 'fro. He's dressed in khakis, a collared shirt, a bow tie, and the shiniest shoes ever. The look on his face screams, "I'm new here. Please be my friend."

Seriously, who wears a bow tie to school?

Swarms of students whiz by, but he stays standing there. And there I am, like an idiot, staring and standing too, when I should be moving. His gaze is a magnet. He smiles at me, and I shoot my eyes straight to the ground. Nosy Julicza notices immediately and just has to give her little two cents.

"Yo, who's that guy checking you out?" She tickles me in the ribs, and I hunch over to stop from laughing.

But when I straighten up to look at him again, he's already disappeared into the sea of students bum-rushing their way through the doors.

NEW SCHOOL, NEW PROBLEMS

"BEATRIZ MENDEZ, PLEASE REPORT to the main office."

I can't even get to homeroom in peace before they're already calling me over the loudspeaker. Funny, because I promised myself that going to Barringer would give me a chance to turn over a new leaf. I'm still gonna be a Diabla through and through, but I'm gonna be as low profile as possible. Do enough to get by.

There's a lot of commotion in the office. The phones are ringing off the hook, the secretaries acting more nervous with each ring. They don't even notice me standing there, even though I'm sure one of them called my name on the intercom.

A man strolls out from behind a wooden door marked "Principal." He might be the tallest guy I've ever seen. Dressed in a three-piece suit, he looks like he's ready to preach at church. He looks over and says, "Are you Beatriz Mendez?"

I nod but don't say nothing.

"I'm Dr. Brown. Come on in," he says.

There's a woman with her back to me seated in one of the chairs. I see her blonde hair and black roots piled up in a loose bun. Scope out those white patent-leather pumps and black stockings. There's only one teacher notorious for that combination: Mrs. Ruiz.

She swings the chair around and twists her mouth into a smile soon as she sees me.

"Your face healed up nicely," she says.

Lies! I want to scream back, but I don't. "What are you doing at Barringer? You were just teaching Spanish at King Middle."

Mrs. Ruiz rises from the chair, leans toward me, then whispers in my ear, "Un nuevo trabajo para mí. Y una nueva escuela para ti. Let's not mess this up, eh?"

Dr. Brown pulls up an extra chair for me near his desk, and we all take our seats.

"Why'd you call me here? Did I do something wrong?" I stare at walls and walls of degrees and awards. Seton Hall University. Yale. The Governor's Award for Leadership. Pictures with the mayor. It's like this man is the freaking president or something.

Dr. Brown speaks first. "Our new guidance counselor, Mrs. Ruiz, had some wonderful things to say about you and her time with you at King Middle School."

My stomach does this little backflip. Wonderful? Doubt it. The last word I would use to describe my time at King Middle is *wonderful*. Mrs. Ruiz must see the *yeah-right* smirk on my face, so she speaks next.

"As I mentioned before, Beatriz has a lot of potential, despite some challenges she recently went through."

Potential? Challenges? Code words for my ass was always in trouble.

"I know about your brother and his gang involvement," Dr. Brown says. "And though I am sorry for your loss, I wanted to—"

"Alleged." I cut him off.

"Excuse me?" he asks.

"Alleged gang involvement. *Sir.*"

I'm not putting my business out there like that. I can see Dr. Brown skimming through that big shiny, bald head of his, searching for how to be firm, but not a total pendejo.

"I looked through your records." He clears his throat. "You were placed a grade behind where you belonged when you arrived from Puerto Rico."

My whole chest rises, thinking for a split second that maybe the school will do right by me. But deep down, I know it's not possible. Not when my report cards are always full of Ds with a side order of Fs.

"I didn't speak much English then, so they held me back a whole year. Why? You gonna put me in my right grade? As you can see, I speak-uh dee English just fine."

Okay, maybe I'm the pendeja for that last part.

Mrs. Ruiz coughs and kicks me with the tip of her heel. Dr. Brown pulls at his tie like he needs to catch his breath.

"Given your grade point average, that's highly unlikely. But what I would like to see is a fresh start for you. Better grades. Complete focus. Think you can do that for yourself?" This guy's all looking me up and down.

Mrs. Ruiz doesn't give me a chance to tell this cabrón where he can stick it. "She can do it. She'll try her best and work hard, right, Beatriz?"

I flash Mrs. Ruiz a fake smile. I still got a soft spot for this lady.

Dr. Brown clears his throat and slaps my file folder on his desk. I already know what's coming next.

"Barringer High School strives to maintain a positive image. We expect excellence from our students. More importantly, this is a drug-free school, young lady, and we'd like to keep it that way," he says as he puts the folder into a drawer.

Yadda, yadda, yadda.

It all goes in one ear and out the other. The funny thing is my best customer at King Middle was Mrs. Caldwell. Claimed that reefer helped with her arthritis. Who knows if that was even true? She slept half the time when she should've been teaching. And when she wasn't sleeping, homegirl had the munchies. But I guess Mrs. Ruiz don't know nothing about that.

"Dr. Brown." I'm tired of his "say no to drugs" speech. "I'm not into that life—drugs, gangs, and such—never was."

Lying and breathing become one.

Mrs. Ruiz clears her throat like she's got a jagged-edged rock caught in there. "Yes, and anyways, that was her brother's life. It's not hers. Right, Beatriz?"

She stares deep into my eyes. I'm not really sure what she's looking for.

"He wasn't into that, either." I try my best to hide the lie in my voice.

"Mrs. Ruiz tells me you're an excellent dancer." Dr. Brown changes the subject.

Bring on the stomach rumbles again. *Can't I just get to class, old man? I got rounds to finish.*

"I used to dance . . . for fun. I don't dance no more . . . anymore, sir."

'Cause I'm too busy taking care of Mami—and reliving the day that took away my brother, the music, and every dream I ever had for myself.

Mrs. Ruiz reaches into her bag and hands me a stack of flyers and applications. I flip through them for a millisecond and see *ballet* and *dance* and *camp* and one paper with *NAACP* in the heading.

That stops me. I remember learning about black identity and the NAACP during Black History Month back in sixth grade. Mr. Pullman even took us on a trip to the Schomburg Center in New York. And as I gazed in awe at all the pictures and stories, he looked me straight in the eye and told me that even though I spoke Spanish, I too was black. And that I should embrace that. Like Celia Cruz, Arturo Alfonso Schomburg, Roberto Clemente, and so many other people featured at the center. It might've been the only time I ever listened in his class, or any class for that matter.

I pull the NAACP flyer from the pile and read it.

Calling all New Jersey high school students of African descent: Register for the Olympics of the Mind with the NAACP ACT-SO competition! Categories include poetry, science, art, dance, and more!

There's more words, but I can't get past the *CP*, and still wonder if I belong. *CP* meaning people of color. I mean technically I'm black, right? No matter how much Abuela tried to deny it when we were growing up. She'd often say,

"No somos moreno porque somos africano. Es porque somos indio." Whenever Abuela said that, Mami would just roll her eyes and tell me not to listen to the crazy old lady. But I still remember Abuela's reason for our family genetics: our bronze skin, broad noses, and pelo malo. Sure, our ancestors were the Taíno people, but there ain't no denying they were African too.

Beyond that, the letters *CP* got me thinking of two more words: can't and possible.

Once upon a time, I would have jumped at something like this. It was almost possible when I joined the pageant at King Middle last year. But I messed that up, got myself kicked out before I even gave myself a chance. And now, with everything that's going on, I can't even dare to dream.

Two feelings break out in a war—hate and loyalty. And honestly, I can't shake either.

"Well, what do you think?" Mrs. Ruiz can't hold in her excitement. "I remember your beautiful salsa dance for the pageant. You can't pass this up. Plus, it looks like it's a free contest." She says *free* like I'm supposed to care.

Money ain't the issue. It's me. And these legs, these arms, this corazón that have lost the will to *feel* the music.

I tuck the papers in the back pocket of my overalls. "Thanks. I'll look into it."

I rise up abruptly, like I'm eager to get to class.

"Remember, Ms. Mendez, bad times don't last forever. If you need to talk, I'm here, and Mrs. Ruiz is available too. I expect to hear great things about you." Dr. Brown gets up too, starts toward the door.

"Sure thing, Dr. Brown," I say quickly. I get ready to bounce out of there.

I make my way out the office door as fast as my feet will go.

The halls are crowded with students shuffling to next period. First stop? Bathroom. The hangout spot. Julicza and Maricela are already in there with a couple of other Diablas, tagging up the walls with our signature pitchfork. I notice the bathroom has trash on the floor and is missing a couple doors on the stalls. Brings me right back to King Middle School.

The crew doesn't see me at first, so I decide to give them a scare.

"Julicza Feliciano, report to the principal's office *now!*"

I never seen that girl hide a can of spray paint so fast. When they all whip around and see it's me, they bust out laughing.

"You scared me half to death, Beatriz!" Julicza is giggling.

"Yo, what's up with getting called to the office earlier?" Maricela is all up in my Kool-Aid.

"Nada importante. But guess who works here now?"

"Shut up, don't tell me. It's Mrs. Caldwell, with her sleepy behind?" Julicza laughs so hard she almost snorts.

"Nope. Mrs. Ruiz. She's a guidance counselor here."

"That's dope. Always liked her. What she want with you?" Julicza asks.

"Just wanted to give me some papers."

"Ooh, for what?" Maricela asks.

"For some stupid fix-my-life camps and a NAACP dance contest."

Maricela's face lights up at the word *dance*, and she starts tugging on my sleeve like a four-year-old.

"Don't even think about it. Those days are done. I already tossed the papers in the garbage."

"Ain't the NAACP for black people? Why would she give you a paper about that?" Julicza asks.

"You don't see that butt? That thing is straight from the motherland." Maricela laughs and smacks me straight on the nalgas.

I laugh and press my hand on my butt cheek to stop the sting.

"My dad's black. I told you that a long time ago, not to mention have you seen my abuela? And quit it, Maricela!" I don't know if I'm playing or if I'm really annoyed.

Julicza stares back at me with twisted lips.

Maricela breaks up the silence. "Y'all, remember what Mr. Pullman used to say? Only difference between black and brown people is where we were dumped off the slave ships."

Some of the other girls start chiming in. "My abuela is black too." "Yo, my papi is blacker than black."

"Whatever, y'all. I got bigger things to do anyway." I cut everyone off.

"Like what?" Julicza asks.

"Like getting back to normal."

"Word, yo, 'cause we missed you like crazy this summer. I mean DQ is holding things down and all, but the Diablos aren't the same without you and our regular meeting spot!" Maricela says.

And Junito. My knees weaken for half a second. I grab the sink to hold me up.

"Yeah, sales were okay. Just not as booming 'cause DQ said we had to lay low during the investigation. Man, I even had to ask my mom for money for school clothes. And she made me ask Ruben for it," Julicza says.

"Ruben?" I ask. "What happened to Dwayne, stepdaddy number four?"

We all look at her, confused as all get-out. It's hard keeping up with Julicza's mom's love life.

"Dwayne lasted all of four and a half seconds. So in comes this new guy, Ruben, stepdaddy número cinco. Mom met him at some festival this summer. Wasted no time moving him in. And this pendejo don't do nothing for free. But he still hooked it up, though." Julicza looks in the mirror, holding up a new tube of red lip gloss.

A dark cloud of worry rises in me. Julicza would never say it, but most of us have a feeling that life at home with her mom's boyfriend of the week isn't all bubbles and rainbows.

"Hey, some guys asked if we wanted to hang out at Frank's Pizzeria after school." Julicza changes the subject.

"That sounds cool. Right, Beatriz?" Maricela jabs me in the ribs.

I let out a little cough. Maricela is forever trying to hook me up with somebody, but it'll never work. All I hear is Junito's voice ringing up inside my head. *No novios. Anything that takes your attention away from the Diablos is dangerous.*

Sometimes when I hear his voice in my head, I want to scream. Pick up the nearest object I can find and throw it. I was supposed to be a loyal sister, even though I found out he didn't follow his own rule.

"You guys go. I gotta help out at the bodega after school."

Before I leave the bathroom, I pull the last nickel bags from my bra and hand them to Julicza. "You think you can handle sales for the juniors? I mean, just for this week?"

Her smile reaches maximum cheese level. "Oh, most definitely!"

She has until Friday to sell them all. She knows the drill.

"And hey, no sampling the product, nena," I remind her as I leave the bathroom to make my next stop.

I spot Tony by the lockers in front of the chemistry lab. He raises his hand and forms it into the shape of a zero over his heart. No need to exchange words. The school day ain't even half over yet, and that boy has already sold off his entire stash. Damn, he's good!

And so fine. Tall with bronze skin and a curly low-fro, but I'd never step to him. He's more like a brother than anything.

I spend the next few periods in English literature (*what's the point of reading Shakespeare, anyway?*), algebra (*useless math I'll never need*), and home economics (*not interested*). Each class only proves the point that I don't need to be here. So as soon as lunch is over, I do what I do best. Cut.

There's an exit door right in the gym. I hesitate for a second when I see a teacher there, but then I notice her slumped over her desk, snoring, drooling, the whole nine. Walking out is easy as one, two, three. I cross the street on the side where the Cathedral Basilica is. There's a statue of la Virgen del Carmen right in front of it. She stares at me like, "Where do you think you're going?"

When I round the corner to walk toward the bus stop, I feel the skin down my back rise up like cactus needles. I look behind me as a sea of cars blasts up and down the street. The hum of the engine of a black car roars louder than the others, closer to my ear than any of them, as it slows down near the bus stop. The vibration ricochets inside me, quickening the pace of my steps. I keep my eyes straight ahead. People park illegally by the bus stop all the time. I walk faster, passing a black Mustang with tinted windows and Bob Marley's "Buffalo Soldier" blasting.

Finally the 25 bus pulls up. I get on and head home to take care of Mami. The Mustang drives beside the bus for three stops before it peels left and speeds down Bloomfield Ave.

I tell myself it's nothing and instead take my mind back to Barringer. I'm not sure that I can carry out a four-year sentence there. This school thing ain't nothing but business for me. So that whole "try your best so you can pass" bit will have to wait. Maybe I'll finish. Maybe I won't.

NIGHTS OF FAME

THE BEATS OF MY HOOD are everywhere. Salsa on Broadway. Rap on Grafton. But these days I block it out and will myself to move forward.

In front of the bodega, Mami is in her usual spot. Milk crate planted in front of the window. Today she gazes at the sky, blue and cloudless, like it's the most fascinating picture she's ever seen. Mami is not alone. Seated next to her is Daniel Martin. Mystery man of Grafton. Never a man of many words . . . except one day last year when I had a run-in with him because of his daughter. Me and him have had bad blood ever since.

I walk up to them, hoping to pull them out of their hypnosis. Mr. Martin pretends he doesn't even see me, even though Mami looks my way.

"¿Tienes hambre, Mami?" I ask. She shakes her head no. I'm hoping she ate something at lunchtime.

DQ and a couple of guys are playing dominoes a few feet away.

"What's up with this picture?" I walk over and ask him.

DQ takes the toothpick out of his mouth and shrugs his shoulders. "Beats me. I ain't seen that man 'round here in a long time. He came to get coffee and a newspaper. Next thing I know, him and Mamadukes been sitting there in silence for like two hours now."

I turn and look at them. For months Mami has worn a look of pain on her face. Somehow, the way she's sitting right there, right now, looks almost peaceful. Like she's caught up in the middle of a prayer. Even Mr. Martin's usual mean mug is looser.

I walk back over to them.

"How's your father-in-law, Mr. Martin?" I ask. Everybody in the neighborhood knows one-and-a-half-legged Pop Pop, grandfather to all of Grafton. He used to love walking up the hill to the bodega to get a cup of coffee and the day's paper, sneaking in a dirty-old-man flirt with Mami. It's been a long time since I've seen him . . . or anyone else from the Martin family, for that matter.

"It's getting harder for him to walk around," Mr. Martin whispers to the sky.

"And what about TJ . . . and your *daughter*?"

Mr. Martin cuts his eyes straight at me. "Better than ever."

The words slice through clenched teeth. I feel it deep in my gut, but I don't say nothing back.

Mr. Martin slaps the newspaper on his knees and rises up. "Nice talking to you today, Mirta," he says to Mami.

She pauses her gaze to look at him, says nothing back, doesn't even crack a smile.

"Wait. She actually talked to you?" I can't remember the

last time I heard Mami's voice. What she said. How she said it.

"Don't always need to move your mouth to tell a story." He starts walking away, not turning around one bit.

DQ and I look at each other, confused as all get-out.

"Come on, Mami, let's get you inside." I help her up.

I check on Abuela and Ms. Geraldine in the bodega to see if they need my help.

"Go," Ms. Geraldine insists. "Liezel is coming after class to help close up."

Hiring Ms. Geraldine and her two daughters was a good decision I made after everything happened.

I help Mami upstairs to our apartment, dress her in a clean bata—this one with the Puerto Rican flag spread all over it—and start making dinner. Most days I ask myself why I even try. Mami doesn't eat like she used to.

Still, I cook to bring the memories back. The times when there was Junito and me and her, and music and dancing and love. I start up a pot of arroz blanco con habichuelas and fry up some chuletas and plantains. Not even the smells pull Mami out of her trance. She's sitting on the couch, eyes glued to this new telenovela—*La pasión de Isabela*. While the rice and beans finish cooking, I sit next to her and hold her hand.

Time passes, the sun starts to go down, and Abuela comes up to the apartment. She showers before joining us at the kitchen table. We sit there like sad puppies, waiting to see how much Mami will eat this time. Half of a nibble of pork chop, about three grains of rice, two beans . . . and she's done.

Typical.

I eat my plateful of food and the rest of hers too.

Also typical.

There is one bright spot in my time with Mami. Once a week. Eight o'clock. Our favorite show, *Fame*, comes on. It's the only time I see Mami look half alive. Not long after we came to Newark, Mami worked like a dog so I could take dance classes at Maria Priadka's in South Orange. Mami swore I had what it took to become a professional, and she convinced Ms. Maria of the same. Deep down, I wanted that for myself too.

Things changed around the time I turned ten. No food, no heat, no future will make you shift your focus real quick. Mami held down three jobs, but it was never enough. Junito was only thirteen, but he found a way to fix it all. That came with secrets, hiding, and me putting my dreams in the back seat.

Last year when I joined that pageant at King Middle, Junito was all like, *That's not a priority, Beatriz!* I remember the hurt like it was yesterday. By that point, we were finally in a better place. The cash flow was good. We had our own bodegas. Food, heat, fresh gear, the whole nine.

But there was nothing Junito could do to stop me from dancing again. Because Mami said so. So every night she worked with me. Re-taught me the dances I'd learned from our island—salsa, plena, bomba—and the ballet, jazz, and ballroom styles I'd learned from Ms. Maria.

Fame's theme song comes on, and Debbie Allen, who plays the dance teacher, Lydia Grant, appears on the screen.

"You got big dreams? You want fame?" She's got this big, booming voice for such a tiny lady. Walking stick in her hand, shoulders squared out in her red cut-off shirt, plus her name is listed in the opening credits as producer. That means she runs shit. You can't tell me that she ain't got a little Diabla inside her too! Any other fan would be all about Jesse or Leroy with their fine selves, or maybe even Coco (she's a brown girl too). But for me, no one but Debbie Allen exists. I swear she is talking to me—her words punching me right in the chest, making me want to scream, *Yes, I do have a dream . . . and this ain't it!*

Abuela can't understand much of the show, but music and dancing are a universal language that makes her just as happy as it makes me and even Mami. For an hour, we all escape to a place where there is no sadness, no loss. Just a group of New York kids using song and dance to burn trouble out of their systems.

When the show is over, Mami and Abuela kneel at the altar in the corner of the living room, praying to a God I'm no longer sure exists. When they're done, I help Mami get to bed. I haven't let her sleep alone since we buried Junito.

The streetlights pour in through the open curtains. I walk over to the window to close them, and see a single car parked by itself with the headlights still on. As soon as I close the curtains, the car pulls off down Broadway.

It doesn't take Mami long to drift away. Once I hear Abuela snoring in the next room, I sneak down the stairs, past the bodega, and straight to the locked storage room in the basement. Years ago Junito told Mami to not rent it out. Made up some lame excuse that he would use it as an art studio. But really it was the meeting spot for the Diablos . . . and a few other hidden activities.

I stand in the middle of the room, looking at the empty

chairs scattered about, willing Junito to come back to me. To us. This Friday will be the first Diablos meeting I've been to since Junito died. He used to run those meetings, and I'd sit and watch him, so in control. I wanted to be everything like that, to have power and admiration that made everyone in the whole neighborhood respect, love, and fear me the way they did Junito.

But now the crown belongs to DQ. Maybe DQ was trying to be nice when he said we could start holding meetings again here. This is what Junito would've wanted anyway. All of us—Diablos y Diablas—together like old times. So I'll spiffy up the room. Put some posters up with our Diablo signature. Add some red decorations to brighten things up. Tag the wall to match my very first graffiti art: ¡Fama! ¡Voy a vivir pa' siempre! Only this time I'll leave off the fame part. I can't have that. At least not now. No such thing as a gangbanger turned famous dancer. But the living forever part? Yeah, I want that. Need that more than ever.

The steps haunt me as I climb back up and into bed with Mami, knowing what comes next. Sleep. Half blessing, half curse. For months now, I've replayed different scenes from my life in my dreams. It's like a mixtape, each song playing out, each dream unfolding in dance, every style I ever learned back in Puerto Rico and here in Newark. And when I get to the end of the tape, my fingers curl to the rhythm, press rewind, and then it starts all over again. I call the album that my dreams have become "Songs in the Key of Dance."

Track One: Dance of the Bomba, 1974
Five years old. Aguadilla, Puerto Rico. Island of my childhood.

Our casita is no bigger than two rooms, with a tin roof that threatens to collapse as soon as a hurricane hits. Aguadilla smells of sunshine and ocean waves and palm trees, and on this day, rain. First as light as teardrops falling from the sky. Not enough to keep me, Junito, and my cousins Elena and Xiomara from jumping rope outside.

> *Mi madre y mi padre*
> *viven en la calle*
> *de San Valentín*
> *número cuarenta y ocho.*

The rain thickens as we continue our schoolyard song. Mami and Abuela run around the yard, grabbing the clothes off the clothesline as we collect raindrops in our mouths and sing to the darkening skies. A car pulls up and it's Papi and my tíos, but we don't stop jumping rope.

> *Mi padre le dice a mi madre,*
> *Señora, toque el piso.*
> *Señora, de una vuelta.*
> *Señora, coja las maletas.*
> *Señora, márchese de aquí.*

Tío Leoncio gets out of the car first, then yells out, "Junior is pretty light on his feet, eh, Juan?"

Through the rain, I can see Papi's deep brown cheeks turn red as he slams the car door behind him. He hobbles over to us, drunk as hell, and yanks Junito from the ropes, mid-jump.

"*Adentro, a la casa . . . ahora mismo.*" Papi orders Junito inside, his voice adding to the rumble of thunder in the sky. Loud and powerful, lighting ready to burn anyone who dares challenge him.

Abuela dumps a pile of clothes in a basket. My cousins drop the rope on the ground and run off to their casita a few doors down from ours.

Papi stumbles into the house, Junito dangling at his side. His scent—a mixture of coconuts and rum—bounces back and forth around the four tin walls.

Mami runs behind him, trying to free Junito from his tight grip.

"*¡Déjalo, por favor!*" she begs, but Papi tosses Junito on the sofa like a rag doll. Junito bites down on his bottom lip, like he's fighting against himself to not scream. That doesn't stop the thick stream of tears coming out of his eyes.

"How many times I have to tell you about ruining my name by playing with girls?" The devil has made its way through Papi. It's not the first time, and I'm sure it won't be the last. So I do what I do best. Hide.

Behind the curtain that splits our casita in two, I see their shadows. I place my hands over my ears. Cover the sounds of the screams, the cries, the threats. None of this exists. Except for the music. The bomba builds inside of me now. I tap my foot silently in counts of four, with the tambor calling back in response, just the way Mami taught me. I twirl to the beat of the drums, the constant swish of the ocean nearby, hypnotizing me with the rhythms.

"You can't keep treating him like this. Just let him be." Mami's voice clashes against my inner song.

Papi throws her against the wall. The tin roof vibrates, threatening to cave in any second.

"I'm not raising a maricón!" Papi yells.

"Enough, Juan! He's only eight years old."

He gives Mami a backhanded slap across the face.

This is normal in our house—Papi doing whatever he wants to Mami and Junito, but never laying a finger on me. Is it because I am his princesa? Is it because he loves me more?

Papi finally turns on the radio to cover his awful words so no one in the barrio hears, though it's already too late. The music fills me up. I want to move and twirl and dance away the ugly. But I can't. Not like this, when Junito and Mami are hurting.

"No te preocupes." Papi lets Junito go and gets all up in Mami's face. "I signed him up for the fights next week. I'll make sure he's not gonna turn out to be a maricón."

The fighting arena is a staple in Aguadilla. Sometimes people fight roosters against each other for money. Other times, it's grown men. And every now and then there are children. Fathers who enter their sons to toughen them up, hoping to score a few bucks and bragging rights. For years Papi threatened that he'd make Junito do it. Now that time is coming, sooner than we'd hoped.

A rumble of thunder echoes above. The vibrations make their way down through the four walls of our casita, spread and fester through Mami, Papi, and Junito, until they finally find me hidden in the shadows.

I wake up gasping, my eyes wildly scanning the room for the family that once was. But there is no Junito and no Papi. I am safe. I think.

A CALL TO ORDER

FRiDay NiGHT COMES FaST. I slip downstairs to make sure everything is perfect as the way I set it last night. Chairs organized neatly against the walls. Long table in the middle of the room.

Whip out Junito's mallet, his favorite way of shutting folks up. Then I start second-guessing myself. I've been away so long. Maybe DQ changed the way things are handled. Will he like the graffiti art I made? Will he think the lemonade and pretzels are stupid? *This ain't a party, princesa. This is business.* I imagine him picking apart my every decision. The tick of the clock tells me I don't have time to worry about none of that.

I prop the back door open with a brick, just like Junito used to do. One by one, everybody'll start to trickle in, while I keep a lookout upstairs.

"¿Que esta pasando?" Abuela catches me stone-cold as soon as I reach the first floor.

"Just gonna hang out with some friends is all." I press

my back to the basement door and look her square in the eye.

Abuela leans in close enough for me to smell the butterscotch candy melting on her tongue. "Yo no soy ciega como tu madre," she warns. "Tengo cuatro ojos."

How is it even possible for an old lady, barely five feet tall, to make me shudder? She's right about one thing. She's not blind like Mami at all. And she's not the only one who's gonna have to keep her eyes open. I gotta make sure her and her four eyes stay outta my business.

"All you see is a group of friends who haven't spent much time together since . . . you know. Necesitamos el apoyo de cada uno." I beg her to understand where I'm coming from.

We need each other. That's my story, and I'm sticking to it. Saying all that is enough for her to walk back into the bodega. Not before giving me the evil eye, though.

I lock the door behind me and the storage room back door too, in case Abuela gets any ideas.

"You sure you ready?" DQ gives me one last chance to change my mind. I feel the silence and everyone's eyes zoned in on me.

"Most definitely. It's time," I say clearly.

"All right mi gente, let's get started!" DQ announces.

Everyone drops their cash on the table, one at a time, while Paco and Fredito count it up. The money stacks higher as each runner gets a nod that they're good to go. All I can think about is how proud Junito would be if he were here right now.

There's a tap on the back door, and for a second I think it's Abuela with her nosy self.

Fredito walks over and looks through the peephole.

"¿Quién es?" I ask, thinking up an excuse to not let Abuela in.

"It's Juan," he says.

Juan Diaz strolls in late, dressed in a Knicks jersey and smelling like he might've broken Diablo rule number three: never get high on the supply. If the smell doesn't give him away, those red-streaked, cloudy-looking eyes of his scream, "Bingo!"

"You're late. Dinero. ¡Ahora!" DQ orders him to pay up.

Juan starts slapping his hands against his chest, searching for pockets that don't exist. He pulls out a wrinkled-up five-dollar bill from inside his boot and slowly places it on the table.

DQ nods his head at me, and I swear I can see fire shoot straight from his ears.

"What happened, bro?" DQ asks.

Juan half laughs, half sniffs. "Didn't have much luck pulling customers this week. I got you next time, though." He wipes the sweat growing on his forehead.

Paco looks at DQ and starts cracking his tattooed knuckles. My stomach does a little spin, remembering what DQ made me promise: if I was gonna come back, I'd have to be a little less princesa and a lot more Diabla.

"We'll *talk* after the meeting," DQ says through clenched teeth.

By now everyone's in their seat, and I know we gotta get started and get done soon, before Abuela really does come looking for me.

DQ stands up and begins. "We now call this meeting to order."

Everyone stands, pounds their chest twice, raises one fist to the sky, and recites, "Blood in, blood out."

Those words have been etched in my mind ever since I was twelve years old.

Everyone sits, and DQ announces, "As you know, a lot of time has passed since we lost our soldier, the original chief of this whole operation."

The room grows real quiet. It's like I can see everyone's face inch downward toward the floor as we relive the memory.

"He was a real leader who made sure we were all taken care of, that our pockets stayed full. But his spirit lives on in me, in you, and in his sister!" DQ's all in his feelings.

Folks start snapping their fingers. It's good to see DQ kept one of Junito's rules. We'd never clap during meetings because Junito didn't want folks upstairs to hear us causing a ruckus.

"To carry out the Diablo legacy, I've picked up where things left off. The older Diablos will handle the sales of all the hard stuff—dope, cocaine, whatever the people want, we got it. Y'all in school, take care of the light stuff—Mary Jane, reefer, weed, whatever you wanna call it—"

"¡Wepa!" One of the guys sings out like it's a party, and everybody starts cracking up.

There's a pull in my stomach, though I laugh along too. It's these drugs that keep food on the table, but in reality, it's those same drugs that took my brother away.

DQ continues. "Word on the street is there's a new strain of reefer coming down the pike, so stay tuned for that. And now that the princesa herself is back in full effect, I'm gonna have her hold down sales at Barringer."

Everybody starts snapping again, and I rise up from my seat to hug DQ, stomach rumbling loud as all get-out.

"Say something," he whispers in my ear. "Make it quick."

I swallow hard and clear my throat. "Um, it's good to be back."

There's more words trapped inside, but that's about all my heart—and DQ—will allow me to say.

"That's my nenaaaaa!" Julicza draws out the "a" extra long.

I take a seat, feeling the red rise in my cheeks.

DQ lays out the plans for us moving forward. "Now that Beatriz is back, she's gonna need a little help holding things down at Barringer. We need two runners for the junior class. Two folks who can keep their nose clean and mouth shut, sell the product, and pile up the stash. A win-win for everyone."

Julicza shoots up out of her chair. "I don't mind taking on that job . . . solo. I'm trying to get out of my mom's crib as soon as I hit sixteen."

Julicza slaps five with Maricela. I smile weakly, knowing that getting out isn't gonna be an option for me no time soon.

A few guys eye Julicza's round backside, and I hear mumbling to the effect of, "You can come stay with me anytime."

Julicza blushes and slowly falls to her seat.

DQ gives Julicza the job and carries on with the rest of the details. "A bit about the 4-1-1 on our setup. Some things might change, but a lot will stay the same. Deliveries on Mondays, drop-offs on Fridays. Once a month, I'll do a New York run to restock, twice if sales are really booming."

My skin shivers hearing all of this. It's a life I've mostly ignored. Let Junito manage stuff, más o menos. As I sit there, I wonder what's going on upstairs in the apartment. Is Mami okay? Does she need me? Maybe I came back too early.

Five months is a long time away, princesa. I can hear Junito in my head.

"As for initiations and compensations . . ." DQ says more, but I don't really hear him because I'm too busy looking at Juan.

He sits in the crowd with his shoulders tight, knees all shaking. His major screw-up tonight means he'll definitely be kissing DQ's fist when it's all said and done.

Through the small basement window, I can see the sky growing dark. Time to wrap things up.

DQ bangs the mallet twice to end the meeting. Everybody grabs the last of the lemonade and pretzels and this week's cut from Paco before heading out through the back door.

Juan files in line right with them, hoping to go unnoticed. But DQ is too quick for that. He reaches for Juan's arm and grips it tight. "You know this was supposed to go down the second you showed your face. It's either now or later, Juan. Later's always worse, though."

"You gotta take it outside," I warn DQ. "Abuela will hear."

"Me?" DQ smirks. "You mean *we*."

My tongue suddenly feels too big for my mouth. Paco opens the back door. Juan gets loose from DQ's grip and goes flying down the alley. But DQ is right behind him. Yanks him by the jersey and slams him to the asphalt, just in time for Paco to catch up.

I don't want to be here. Don't want to see what comes

54

next. But it's too late. DQ and Paco are already taking turns punching Juan, throwing threats with each blow.

"You don't come up in here without my money." DQ is ferocious, thick veins weaving from his neck to his bald head.

I stand in the alley, watching each hit, until DQ throws me a look that says, *Get in here, now!*

Next thing I know, I'm doing as I'm told. Arms flying, fists tossing, feet stomping Juan in perfect rhythm with Paco and DQ. Blood sprays from Juan's mouth, some landing on my shirt, some spraying on a cluster of wishmaker flowers sticking out of the asphalt. It's a scene that brings up unwanted memories for me: the fights and beatdowns I've ordered over the years—one in particular that I still think about to this day—and of course, Friday the thirteenth. The sound of fists on bone, the click of a trigger, the sirens screaming over my voice as I called Junito's name.

I'm starting to sweat, and whatever I've eaten today is slowly rising up from my gut. Any second I'm gonna blow. I can't do this. Not right now. Not when the memories are still too raw.

"Stop it! Enough!" I push DQ against the brick wall, which makes Paco stop immediately.

Juan dares not whimper. Not a single tear. He just lies in the fetal position, each breath fighting against the next.

"Let him go!" I order them both.

Paco lifts Juan, with his torn-up jersey, and shoves him down the alley toward Broadway. Even though Juan stumbles with each step, the world continues to move. Cars zip by and people walk past, ignoring the bloody sight.

"What was that all about?" The corners of DQ's mouth are doused in spit.

"I think we need to rethink initiations and compensations. Find another way, you know?" I say, not looking at DQ.

"Who are you, Beatriz? Dr. King or something? You're the girl who was always down for a good fight. How soon you forget the beatdown you ordered last year. Grafton Ave. Top of the hill. The Diablos against TJ—and his fat cousin, that wannabe beauty-queen chick, got in the mix. What was her name again?"

I really do feel like I'm gonna throw up. "Stop it! Just . . . stop talking, DQ."

DQ zips up his jacket and starts to walk away, but not before getting in one last jab. "Let's not forget who's in charge now, Beatriz."

I stand there, alone in the alley, trying my best to forget the me I once was, trying to figure out the me I still am. Truth is, I'm not sure I like either one.

GAME OF LIES

"SO YOU THINK YOU CAN just roll up in here after missing nine days of school when the month's not even over yet?" Dr. Brown is giving me a look I don't like.

Even though I'm across his big wooden desk, I can feel the steam rolling off his tongue. I'm sitting in the chair, slouching, my body language showing every bit of *I don't care, bro*.

I been here all right, for drop-offs. In and out before the bell even rings to let the students in.

"Sit up, young lady, when I'm speaking to you!" He throws more fire into his voice.

Mrs. Ruiz gives me a pinch on my elbow, and I do it. Just for her, though.

"Where have you been?" By this point he's having a by-himself conversation.

Hustling this reefer. That's what I really want to say.

"Sick." Somebody oughta give me an award. My fib game is tight.

Mrs. Ruiz tries to calm the situation. "Do you have a doctor's note, Beatriz?"

"Oh, no, we don't believe in doctors." I thicken my accent and add to the lie. "My family comes from a long line of curanderas."

Dr. Brown looks confused as hell while Mrs. Ruiz explains to him how certain cultures believe in healing the body through the earth and not with modern medicine. I'm smart enough to know that the principal questioning my spiritual and cultural practices is a no-no.

I ain't been staying at school because I got better things to focus on. Like supply and demand. It hasn't been easy lying to Abuela, though. Every day when I head out in the morning, she thinks I'm going to school. I been going—to check on my runners. And on days when I stay home, I just make up any old holiday to say that school is closed. Yesterday was National Rap Song Observance Day. Next week it'll be something else.

"Well, now that you're feeling better, I'm going to need you to come to school more often if you expect to make it to tenth grade," Dr. Brown says seriously.

I can't control the little smirk that grows on my face.

"Oh, you think this is funny?" Dr. Brown says.

"No, sir." *I think school is a complete waste of time, actually.*

"Perhaps I'll need to conduct a home visit with your parents."

Boy, that smirk fades faster than a dying cigarette butt. The last thing I need is Dr. Brown rolling up on my operation so he can get a peek at my spaced-out mom sitting on a milk crate, staring at the ground. Or even worse, see her having imaginary conversations with Mr. Martin. Nope. I'm good.

"I called your former school, you know." He clears his throat and waits for me to react.

Here we freaking go.

"And?" I try my best not to suck my teeth.

"And I know about the fight you set up against a Barringer graduate last year. I surely hope that you have evolved, young lady."

Eighth grade is like a permanent stain on my rep. Mrs. Ruiz shifts in her seat, looking all uncomfortable. There's no way she ratted me out.

"You don't have to worry about me or any fights or my attendance. I'm back and feeling better. And I hope you won't judge me on what happened in the past . . . sir." I almost want to believe that last part.

Dr. Brown fastens the buttons on his jacket as he rises. "Let's just try to have a good school year."

Mrs. Ruiz nudges me to stand. "She will, Dr. Brown. We'll schedule some appointments to get her on track. I'm thinking the peer tutoring program might be good for her."

I return Mrs. Ruiz's smile but whisper in my head, *En tus sueños.* I have zero time for some program.

Together we walk out of the office, not saying a word. I can smell the disappointment steamrolling off of Mrs. Ruiz's shoulder-padded blazer.

As soon as Dr. Brown's door closes behind us, she whips me around hard to face her, just like Mami used to do when she was mad at me.

"Esta es tu oportunidad. Don't blow it!" She gets right up in my face.

I see that look in her eyes. The hope fading. And for a split second, I don't like it. Especially since she had my back in there. It's the same look Mami gave me when she noticed I was spending less time on the dance floor and more time with Junito and his "friends."

Mrs. Ruiz sashays her way toward the guidance office, that purple blazer floating behind her like eagle wings.

I hear a voice behind me. "Well, that's quite the strut Madame Ruiz has. What'd you do to make her incensed?"

It's homeboy with the bow tie from the first day of school, with a mixed-up French-Jamaican sounding accent. Looking like a staff member with his business suit, tie, and those shiny-ass black shoes. He leans in and stares deeper in my eyes, all up in my business.

"And you are?" I ask, moving the blade around my inner cheek with my tongue.

He cracks a smile, stands up real tall, and shows off the broadest pair of shoulders I've ever seen on a nerd.

"Just making conversation." He extends his hand to shake mine, but I don't return the favor.

"The name's Nasser." He pushes his hand into his pocket. "I'm new here, from Miami. Junior class."

The way he speaks is different but somehow familiar.

"Nasser? Is that Arabic or something? Is that why you talk funny?" I don't even try to be polite.

"Ah, you know your etymology."

What the heck is that? Some kind of disease? "Come again, bro?"

He laughs, and all of a sudden I feel three levels of stupid. "Word origins, like where names come from. Mine means 'victorious one.' What about your name?"

I didn't hear what he said because I'm staring at his smile the whole time. This dude's got the whitest teeth I've ever seen, surrounded by a pair of fluffy lips. Not too big, not too small. And in my head, I'm asking him the dumbest question ever. *What kind of toothpaste do you use?*

"Have I said something wrong?" Mr. Arm & Hammer knocks me out of my thoughts.

"Huh?"

"Your name? Unless asking is a crime or something."

My skin turns uncomfortably hot, and I start to wonder if he sees the same face I still see when I look in the mirror. Doesn't matter how much time has passed. One side is permanently larger than the other. My hand finds its way toward my hair, and I shift it forward to cover what I don't want him, or anyone else, to notice. I don't have time for this right now. The bell's about to ring.

"Beatriz . . . Beatriz Mendez."

"Ahhh. *Bee-ah-treez.*" Nasser pronounces it in a perfect accent. "Derived from the late Roman, meaning 'voyager' or 'traveler.'"

My whole body ignites, and I have no clue why. Then Nasser flashes that white, expensive-toothpaste smile, and it circles its way around his face.

"Yeah, traveler, that's me." The bell screams, and my fingers start to tap the air. "And on that note, looks like I need to be *traveling* to class."

"I'll see you around, *Bee-ah-treez.*" He says something else, but the hallway fills with students and chaos. The noise and the movement and the rhythm of it all swallows me, and Nasser's words, whole.

FAME WANNABES

I DECIDE TO STAY at school for the rest of the day, especially since fire-breathing Brown's got his mal de ojo on me. Every single class is teaching garbage that I'll never use when I'm an adult. Polynomials? Dumb. Citizenship? I'm already a citizen.

Somehow I survive until last period. I stop at my locker because I left my schedule there. Had I been coming to school for the past two weeks, I would've had it memorized already. I take a look at my last class: mixed gym. In other words, some intensified version of hell . . . featuring boys and girls from different grade levels . . . in matching Barringer Blue Bears gym uniforms. Aren't I so lucky?

I head to the girls' locker room to get dressed. The second I put on those tight, booty-showing shorts I already know how this is gonna end. With me slipping out when no one is looking.

When I get to the gym, it's packed with at least forty students. A swarm of butts and balls suffocating in

these god-awful shorts. And then there's Mrs. Howard—
way too frumpy, with long, stringy hair and dressed in
sweatpants, a hoodie, and heels. Is it me or do all gym
teachers look like they've never actually been to the
gym?

"Okay, ladies and gentlemen, for the past couple weeks
our theme was volleyball. For the next couple of weeks,
we'll move on to social dancing, so no need for sneakers.
Bring your dancing shoes to the next class."

My heart stops at that word: *dancing*. There is no
way on God's green earth that I'm gonna dance in gym.
Not with my big behind looking like it's snacking on
my shorts. Not when the last time I danced was Friday
the thirteenth. Dancing no longer exists in my world.
Besides, it ain't even a sport. Shouldn't we be playing
basketball or something?

I'm sitting on the bleachers, scanning the exit behind
Mrs. Howard and planning how I'm gonna leave without
this woman seeing me. I promise myself that the second
everybody gets up and she turns her back, I'm out.

I tried, Dr. Brown, I really did.

But Mrs. Howard stands there, pushing up her glasses
on her nose. Then she turns the page on her clipboard and
announces, "I'll be mixing you up by grade and gender."

Some of the students look happy. Some look terrified.
I ain't gonna lie. I'm one of them.

"Today we shall waltz." Mrs. Howard gestures for one
of the students to press play on the boom box.

A flute pipes through the speakers, followed by the
sounds of violins and sparkles and freaking fairy dust. It's the
most boring music I've ever heard in my life. And judging

by the looks of some of the students around me, they feel the same way.

"Ahh, 'The Blue Danube' by Strauss." Mrs. Howard starts talking in a British-sounding accent and does the most awkward by-herself dance.

And it's all . . . just *wrong*. The feet, the hand positioning, everything. I know I'm out of practice, but I could get up there and do a better job.

In walks Dr. Brown, making his usual "survey the school" rounds. I know that principals do that every day, but so far this man has poked his head into three of my classes. Straight stalking me, yo!

The high part of the song squeals. Mrs. Howard and Dr. Brown start to dance together . . . or should I say try to dance. If this is a waltz, I want no part of it.

Dr. Brown scans the bleachers, sees me sitting there, and throws me a satisfied "nice to see you in class" smile.

It doesn't look like escaping is an option at the moment. Dr. Brown spins Mrs. Howard into a dip, and they do a curtsey and bow as the song ends. The students erupt in applause, even though we all know they both looked ridiculous.

Mrs. Howard looks at us. "That's all you have to do, students. Just flow with the music. And try not to step on each other's toes."

I wanna scream so bad: *That's not how Debbie Allen and the kids on* Fame *do it. There's more to it than that, lady!* But I stay quiet. I've already gotten in enough trouble for the day.

Dr. Brown waves at us and walks out of the gym. ¡Gracias a Dios!

"First pair up is *Queen* Shakira Danielle Williams and *King* Michael Jermaine Ivery." Mrs. Howard calls out everyone's first, middle, and last names, throwing in a royal ranking to, I don't know, make us feel special? A *duke* here, a *duchess* there. I get that she's trying to stay in character and get us all excited, but this woman is plain loca.

A different classical song starts playing, making me want to fall asleep.

One by one, I see the students pair up until the bleachers empty out, and it's just me sitting at the top and some dude with a business jacket over his uniform, way down in the first row. Wait, is that Mr. Arm & Hammer?

"*Princess* Beatriz Ayita Mendez"—Mrs. Howard pronounces my middle name all kinds of wrong—"and *Prince* Nasser Kervin Mo . . . ree . . . aw . . ."

"Moreau." Nasser stands, pushes his glasses up, and looks my way. "Derived from the French, meaning 'the dark one.'"

Oh, heck no! I'm not being paired up with Señor Sabe'todo.

Everybody is staring at me and the guy who thinks he knows everything. I let out a sigh that no one but me hears as I drag my feet down the bleachers.

"Okay, everyone lock hands."

Then Mrs. Howard turns up the music, looking like she's trying to impersonate Debbie Allen. She's got the neck going, the fingers snapping. But she is *waaay* too uncoordinated (and white!) for that.

"Now begin. Feel the music." She lifts her arms in some horrible attempt at a ballerina pose.

At first students are laughing, but it doesn't take

them long to at least try. Nasser places both hands on my shoulders, and I stand there, refusing to touch him back.

"It'll be fine." He flashes me a smile. "Come on, at least try. We don't have to be any good. I mean, look at the teacher."

But I don't move an inch. I vowed to never dance again. I just don't have it in me. Plus the song is straight boring. Who dances to this stuff?

Mrs. Howard walks over to us. "Is there a problem here?"

I'm expecting Mr. Goody Two-shoes to rat me out, but instead he says, "Oh, no, doing just fine. We're discussing our movements. . . . Right, Beatriz?" He rolls the *r* in my name like it's second nature.

Mrs. Howard must believe him, because she walks away and doesn't even look back. Fine by me. She's got thirty-eight other kids who need her attention anyway.

"You know, with a name like yours, I bet you have dance in your blood." Nasser removes his hands from my shoulders.

"I thought you said *Beatriz* means 'traveler' or something like that."

"Give me a second," he says, running out the gym doors and straight toward the boys' locker room.

"Yo, what're you doing?" I call after him, but he doesn't hear me.

So I just stand there, arms folded, foot tapping impatiently, while everyone dances around me looking dumb as hell. A minute later, here comes Señor Sabe'todo, breathing heavy, with a bible-size book clutched to his chest.

With the music dancing between us, Nasser starts flipping through the pages like mad.

"I knew it! I knew your middle name was special."
Homeboy is way too excited.

"And let me guess . . . *Ayita* means 'dance.'"

Nasser shakes his head and laughs in tune with the
violins. "According to my etymology book, the history isn't
entirely clear, but it seems it might mean 'first to dance.'
It could also be a style of Nigerian dance. Either way, both
have to do with dancing. See?"

I lean into the page to see for myself.

"Yeah, I used to dance a long time ago, and I was the first
in my family to take real dance classes. But it's not my thing
anymore. Plus, I knew that's what *Ayita* means anyway."

And the award for best liar goes to . . .

Nasser places the book on the floor and starts laughing.

"What's so funny?" I ask.

"Nothing." I can hear the cover-up in his voice.

I cross my arms tighter and give him the stare of death.

"Well, it's just that Mrs. Howard is trying real hard to
turn this gym dancing experiment into my favorite TV
show."

"What's that?" I ask.

"Promise not to laugh?" I swear I see a sparkle in Nasser's
eyes.

"I won't. Now spit it out."

"*Fame.*"

That one word changes my whole spirit. "Yo, that's my
joint too! Debbie Allen plays the heck out of Lydia Grant."
I don't know why, but my feet lift up on their toes a little.

Mrs. Howard lowers the music, and the class stops
dancing. "Okay, that's enough for today. The new physical
education curriculum added social dancing as a form of

exercise. So even though I may not be the best dancer—don't get me wrong, back in the day I could do a mean Lindy Hop—we'll just have fun with this. You don't have to be any good. All you gotta do is show up and move, and you'll get a passing grade."

The students clap in relief. I do too, since this might be the only class I actually pass. Assuming I keep coming, that is.

The bell rings, and I walk back to the locker room to change out of these uncomfortable shorts. Once I'm done, I start making my way out the school exit, and I see Maricela and Julicza on the sidewalk with at least five other Diablas waiting at their side.

"Hey, Beatriz, wait up." Nasser runs after me, and I stop short as the sea of students continues to walk past us.

"Why don't you dance anymore?" he asks.

"Long story," I spit out fast. Dude is nosier than Abuela.

"You should think about getting back into it. I dance too, you know."

My mind flashes back to Aguadilla. Waves crashing against the sand. Me, seven years old. Junito, ten. Family beach barbecue. Salsa blasting from the radio. And Junito trying to dance . . . with a boy from the barrio. Papi loses his cool.

"*Boys don't dance with boys.*" The memory of Papi's voice booms me back into the present.

"So let me get this straight. You're into word origins, you like to watch *Fame*, and you know how to dance?" This guy can't be for real.

"Poetry is my thing too. Oh, and playing the guitar

and cooking. But shhh . . . don't say any of that out loud."
Nasser leans in closer.

"Why not?"

"I don't need all these Barringer ladies trying to hunt a brother down." His wink lights me up. But that only lasts a split second, because I know better.

"Well, isn't that what most guys want?" I say, searching his eyes for the tiniest clue that he's full of mierda.

Nasser doesn't flinch one bit. "Al contrario."

I swear I feel a slow burn start up right in my chest.

"The poetry, the books I read, the dancing, I'm doing all of that for personal growth. My parents say every little skill I learn will look good on those college applications next year."

College? I can't even think that far in advance. "I mean, if you like to dance, that's pretty dope."

"Say, there's this thing . . . coming up with the N double A—"

Nasser is cut off when Maricela calls out to me. "Yo, Beatriz, it's about to rain. Vámonos, nena!"

She and the rest of the Diablas are already halfway down the block.

"What were you trying to say? The end of a double what?" I face Nasser again. Those brownish, green-gold eyes pierce right through me.

"Nothing. Nothing important," he admits.

It begins to grow dark and cloudy. A bolt of lightning pierces the sky.

"Um, I gotta go."

"See you later, Beatriz *Ayita* Mendez."

I refuse to smile at this guy. Instead I run to catch up

with my girls, and we cross the street toward the cathedral and head up the block to catch the bus.

Black and brown kids gather in crowds to make their way home before the storm comes. We only got like a handful of white kids at Barringer. We're mostly black and Hispanic, all with hair and eyes and skin in shades of brown and browner. Ahead, tucked deep into the crowd, I notice something that brings back a memory I pushed down so far and deep, I'd almost forgotten about it until now.

Yellow shirt. Yellow bandana. Long, blonde dreads.

I don't know what comes over me. My feet rush me forward like propellers on a plane. Next thing I know, Julicza, Maricela, and the rest of my crew are following me through the crowd. My tongue moves my blade until it pierces my flesh. I taste blood as a drop trickles down my throat. But I don't care.

I'm running fast now, and so is the yellow bandana. Past the supermercado, past Frank's Pizzeria, the wave of people still huddled around me, and the yellow scarf drifting farther and farther. When the thickness clears out, I see nothing but an empty street.

The girls stop running, huffing and puffing like they haven't exercised in years.

"What was that all about, Beatriz?" Julicza asks.

"And what's up with the bloody lip?" Maricela says.

I wipe my mouth with my sleeve. The number 25 bus pulls up.

"Nothing. I thought I saw someone I knew."

BEATRIZ VS. BEATRIZ

THERE'S aN aRGUMENT PLaYiNG out inside my head. Beatriz vs. Beatriz, and I'm not sure who's gonna come out victorious.

Me: Was that who I think it was?

Me: Lots of girls wear dreadlocks. Hello, it's 1984! It's a style.

Also me: Ice-blonde dreads. Yellow bandana. Wake up, girl!

I've spent the past five months half dead, half fighting with myself. Do I open my mouth and tell everybody what really happened in the abandoned lot? And if so, what would DQ do? Start another war? Have me and Mami dodging bullets all over again? And what if he ain't around this time?

Get it together, Beatriz.

Yeah, I'm just trippin'. The papers say the Macoutes are done. So do the streets.

By the time the 25 rolls up in front of the bodega, the rain is coming down hard. Mami is in her usual spot.

Mr. Martin is sitting right next to her, holding an umbrella large enough for both of them.

Mr. Martin has a notebook in his hand, and he's reading as Mami searches the sky for the sun. I stop and listen.

There comes a time when tears turn to dust,
rising like ashes, hot and dry.
And so she'll wait, hope and pray,
for smiles, laughter, and songs of yesterday.

When he finishes, Mami looks at me and smiles. For a moment I feel the good memories of long ago. When it was the three of us, braving it together when we first got here from Puerto Rico. I stand there, not knowing how to process what I'm feeling. All I know is there's something in my eyes causing them to fill with water, and it's not the rain.

Mr. Martin rips a sheet of paper from his notebook and says, "Here's another one to read . . . when you need it." Mami slips it in the pocket of her bata, like it's one of those expensive wooden saints from Puerto Rico. Then Mr. Martin hands her the umbrella.

She's still staring at me like something in that poem made her wake up. Mr. Martin, not caring about the rain coming down so thick, starts walking away. Like he always does whenever I turn up.

"Mr. Martin!" I run after him, rain pounding against my face. "Who wrote that?"

"I did." He turns around and looks me square in the eye. That dark skin, the space around his mouth, creased with streaks of mean. That's the man I knew from the way his daughter explained it to me when we were friends. Not this poetry-writing, Langston Hughes wannabe. Something is up.

"I don't get why you keep comin' around here. I did

what I did almost a year ago. If you're trying to rat me out to my mom, now's not the time." I can't help telling him off.

"Funny how you say that so cool and calm. What you *did* was order your little punk-ass friends to jump my nephew, but your mom don't know nothing 'bout that. And it ain't my job to tell her. Like you said, she got enough to deal with."

"You think you're helping my mom with your stupid poems and your sky gazing? Well, there ain't nothing you can do to fix her." I raise my voice a little.

"I'm not trying to *fix* or help her. She got you for that. Shame you don't see it yet."

I stand there, rain soaking through my clothes, trying to think of something else nasty to say, but there's a tug in my gut. Tells me to simmer down, if only for a moment.

"What do you mean?"

Mr. Martin doesn't even answer. He just presses forward and turns left, making his way down Grafton Hill to the projects.

When I get back to the bodega, DQ has already taken Mami upstairs to our apartment.

Before I can even climb the steps, Abuela appears in the hallway out of nowhere, scaring the living daylights out of me.

"You can't just sneak up on people like that!" I say. "¿Qué pasa, Abuela?"

And like a scene from a horror movie, she leans in all close, and I swear her eyes change color.

"Dime con quién andas, y te diré quién eres." She speaks through tightened lips.

Here we go again with Abuela's out-of-nowhere warnings. What the hell does she mean, "Tell me who you hang around with, and I'll tell you what you're about"? She must be talking about DQ.

Honestly, she didn't like him from the second she met him, and the reasons just keep piling up the longer she stays. He has tattoos all over his body. He chews with his mouth open. And the best one of all: es un cobarde.

She thinks he's a coward for leaving Junito. For running into the bodega when the bullets flew through the air that day. Doesn't acknowledge that he got Mami out of harm's way.

And as usual I stand there and take it all in. Let the old lady have her say until she tires of talking to my brick exterior. It's not until she turns her back to me and walks into the bodega that I head upstairs.

Mami is already seated on the couch, wrapped in a blanket. DQ lit the candles at the altar, and Mami stares and stares at the glow. Lips moving, probably saying a prayer, but not a sound escapes. I wonder if she's reciting Mr. Martin's poem.

"What's your take on this guy sitting outside the bodega with Mami like that? Reading her poetry too?" I ask DQ.

"At first I had a problem with him hanging with her. Like homeboy is pretty weird, you know? But then I figured maybe he's lonely. His daughter bounced off to some boarding school. His nephew went away too. You took care of that." DQ laughs and holds up his hand for a high five.

I'm not so sure I'm proud of that anymore, but I slap his hand anyway.

"But seriously, I see the way your mom is when he's with her. It's like she mourns a little less. Maybe it's good for her."

"Yeah, I guess you're right," I agree.

I grab DQ's hand to walk him to the kitchen so Mami won't hear. "We're good, right? I mean that argument over Juan . . ."

"I get that you ain't been around in a while, but there's no negotiating when it comes to mistakes. Every move deserves a strategy. That's where Junito messed up."

Pain sharpens in the space between my eyes. DQ's hand is on my shoulder, heavy as lead, with no sign of warmth or cold running through his fingertips.

He keeps talking. "Listen, I gotta do what I gotta do to keep this operation tight, even if it means reminding people who's in charge. We're finally in a good place. The cops ain't sniffing 'round no more. And now that all this time has passed by, it's time to up our game on the streets and behind bars."

That last part stings a little.

"What are you gonna do, DQ?" I cross my arms, dig my nails into my damp skin.

"Something I've been waiting to do for a long time." DQ smirks.

I hang on to DQ's every word, images forming in my mind. The heat of that dude's breath, the shivering effect of his words—new pop blay—and that bow. Deep, dramatic, knees bent in perfect form. And the ice-blonde dreads.

"You *do* want this handled, right? The timing is right. I already got our Diablos in lockup on alert. They're just waiting for my word."

My shoulders begin to shiver. "Haven't we got enough blood on our hands?" I ask.

"Sometimes blood is needed to send a message."

I look up at DQ, feel my eyes start to water up, but I don't want him to see me like that. So I bury my face in my hands and force myself to breathe. Inhala, exhala.

This whole time away from the Diablos, I shifted my focus, watched DQ do all the things Junito did and more. Is this what DQ wanted all along? To be the one in charge? But then I shake those thoughts out of my head real quick. DQ ain't been nothing but good to me and this family. No matter what Abuela says with her old-school island thinking.

I consider telling DQ about the girl I saw after school, but maybe I really was trippin'. Sleep hasn't exactly been my friend these days. But I decide not to.

I let DQ out and settle in for my nighttime Monday routine. Make dinner—piñón, Mami's famous Puerto Rican lasagna; green salad; and flan for dessert—and wait for Abuela to come upstairs from the bodega. Together we'll eat and watch Mami pretend to eat. This time a little more than the last, we can only hope. Flip on the television at eight o'clock to watch *Fame.*

Take in the magic and wonder that is Debbie Allen. Lose myself in the way she moves. It's like her every arabesque and pirouette become a necessary part of being alive. I imagine what my life would be like if I had a teacher like that. Someone who could see the dreams building up inside me. But instead all I see is myself, sitting in the four corners of my home, wishing for what could've been. And I see the glow in Mami's eyes for that whole hour too, like she's right there, stuck in the vision with me. But it's my eyes that glow when this week's episode ends with a picture of Debbie and the cast and a voiceover announcement.

Calling all tri-state area dancers! Do you like to dance? Do you want fame? Audition to be an extra on the hit show *Fame*! Open to ages 13 to 25, all experience levels welcome! Auditions will be held Friday, November 9, 1984, at 7:00 p.m. at the Haaren High School building, 10th Ave. & 59th St., in Manhattan.
Join us for an opportunity of a lifetime!

Mami squeezes my hand real tight and looks at me with desperate eyes.

Translation: *You have to go, Beatriz.*

"¿Que dicen ellos en la televisión?" Abuela wants me to translate.

"Nada importante." I'm not getting into it with her, so I hop up from the couch and flick the television off before that nosy old lady asks anything else.

Track Two: Dance of the Plena, 1976
Tonight's dream fast-forwards two years from the last one.

I sit across from Abuela, Mami, and Junito at the table, squirming as Mami applies ice to Junito's bloody mouth. It swells larger with each passing moment.

It took some time, but as promised, Papi signed Junito up for the street fights, knowing he never stood a chance. Each loss gets harder, wears down the confident, carefree Junito I once knew. It's like a little piece of him dies every time he loses. The pain of seeing Papi walk away from the fighting square in disgust. The agonizing silence of seeing Junito walk through that door, alone and broken.

"Mami, can you take me to a doctor?" Junito asks, wincing in pain.

"Nonsense." Mami applies ice to the split on Junito's top lip. "These are just a few scrapes."

"Not for that, Mami. To fix me. Como estoy por dentro." Junito places his hand over his heart.

Mami stands upright, bringing the ice pack with her.

"Juan Luis Mendez"—she always says his full name when she's mad—"there is nothing inside *of you that's broken. You hear me?"*

"Then why does Papi call me a maricón? If you take me to a doctor, lo cura todo, yes?" Junito asks as his rib cage deflates.

"There's no such . . . well . . . it's not a disease. . . ." Mami stumbles through each word.

Junito lifts his face to meet Mami's eyes. "But I am gay, right?"

"Am I a maricona?" I chime in, too young to know what I'm really saying. Not fully understanding the meaning behind the word, the hurt that comes with it.

Mami and Abuela exchange hardened looks.

Abuela says, "Hush, the both of you. You don't know what you are yet, or what you will be in life."

"Ooh, ooh, I know! ¡Quiero ser bailarina!" I get up and do a pirouette.

That makes Junito smile, just a little.

"And it doesn't matter what you are or aren't," Abuela adds. "It only matters that you're a good person with a pure heart."

Junito sighs.

"Don't worry about your father, mi'jo," Mami says.

"Maybe if I change, Papi will love me?" Junito looks at Mami and then at Abuela.

Neither of them answers. Abuela grabs Mami by the shoulder and pulls her away from us so we don't hear what she says or does next. Little does she know, I have bionic eyes and ears.

Abuela pulls out something from the bra under her bata. A brown envelope. Thick with green, stacked like an American dream. Those crisp, new dollar bills make their way down from Mami's water-filled, fist-cushioned eyes and straight into her pale, shaking hands.

"Mirta, you can't go on like this. . . ."

Abuela's warning plays on repeat. Each time ringing louder and louder.

My eyes open and all I'm left with is Mami's silhouette in the moonlight. She's sitting up in the bed next to me, hunched over, face buried in her knees, whimpering softly.

"It's okay," I whisper through the darkness. "You just had a bad dream."

And I'm not really sure if I'm saying that to her . . . or to myself.

FINDING MY WAY

ALMOST TWO MONTHS IN, and I think I've figured out how to manage going to school while keeping Dr. Brown off my back. It turns out the security guard, Raymond, has himself a little reefer habit. And who better to supply him with the good stuff than the princesa? He hooks me up by letting me leave without ratting me out, or sometimes if I show up late, he lets me in through the auditorium door.

We got an understanding, the two of us. Keep our mouths shut and we both get what we need. Keeping a low profile is the way to go. Most of the teachers take attendance by passing around a sign-in sheet. There's at least a couple of Diablas in all my classes, so they cover for me when I'm not there. Besides, the classes at Barringer are so overcrowded, half the time I doubt the teachers even notice.

Halloween's coming up, and everyone's all excited. They got the school decorated with posters for the Halloween dance on the twenty-sixth. I have zero intention of going, even though most of the Diablos are gonna go. Just before the last period of the day, I stop at my locker. The halls are empty, and the bell hasn't rung yet.

I see a guy walking down the hall toward me, and what do you know, it's Señor Sabe'todo. He's wearing a bow tie and argyle sweater, looking good and ready to recite some hard-to-pronounce word, probably derived from some country I never heard of.

"Always a pleasure to run into you, Beatriz *Ayita*." I smell him before he even reaches me. Soapy, pine-tree-like, intoxicating. And suddenly I can't remember the combination to my locker.

I don't have time for this right now. "Yeah . . . hey."

"Miss me in gym?" he asks, and I got no clue what he's talking about. It's been a good while since I've been to that class.

"Um, yeah." I shrug.

"Guidance transferred me out of gym to honors math. Had enough PE credits from my last school. But I do miss dancing with you. Well, trying to, at least."

He smiles that too-white smile, and I swear my cheeks start turning red.

"Are you sick or something?" Nasser asks.

I drape a thick handful of hair over my face. My eyes scan the floor, looking for something to say. For some reason, I'm acting all punk-like, and I can't stand it one bit.

"No, not sick. Just . . . busy. And you're right, gym isn't the same without you."

"Well, if that's the case you're really gonna miss me during the last two marking periods."

"Oh yeah?" I smirk. "Why's that?"

"Mrs. Ruiz has a few of the honors students applying

for college prep classes at Rutgers downtown, so if I get accepted, I'll be there a few days a week. By the time I graduate from Barringer, I'll already have some college credits."

Of course.

"I've been meaning to ask you something," he says.

I look at my watch. Time is money. "Sure. What's up?"

"I was checking out some of the other programs in the guidance department, and I saw this." Nasser flashes the flyer Mrs. Ruiz gave me on the first day of school. The one about the NAACP. It says ACT-SO Competition on it.

"You said you used to dance. You should go for it," Nasser says.

Yeah, that. Confusion and desire start a secret battle inside me, and suddenly I blurt out, "Look, I don't have time for—"

"Ain't nobody here gonna give you a chance."

The earth stops turning on its axis. "Excuse me?"

Nasser moves in close to my face, all dramatic, and starts walking in circles around me in his shiny penny-loafer shoes. "You've got to take your chance, if you've got guts," he says in a low voice.

That's when I realize this boy is quoting from the first episode of this season of *Fame*!

"Oh, I got guts, all right!" I play along. "I got more guts than anybody in this whole doggone school."

Nasser's breathing blends in with mine as he struggles to remember the next line. His staredown lasts for all of three seconds before we both lose it. He laughs. I follow. And for that short moment, life feels so good.

"Did you see the call for auditions on TV? *Fame* try-outs are coming up on November ninth," Nasser says.

I'd blocked that out of my head since I heard the announcement on television a few weeks ago. Avoided Mami's every-now-and-then pleading eyes, the excited whispers at school.

"Come on . . . this is *Fame*. I know I'm not missing it. You shouldn't either, *Ayita*."

The way he says my middle name makes my blood race. But I can't tell if that's good or bad.

"Well, I haven't danced in a while. I'm too rusty." I throw in that excuse to seal the deal.

"Tell you what. Come take a dance class with me downtown this Friday. You can practice for the audition there."

"But Fridays are . . ." *Gang meetings.* I seal that last bit in my mouth.

"This is *Fame*. . . . You know, Debbie Allen, Gene Anthony Ray, Janet Freaking Jackson! You said you used to dance, right?" He's getting all hyped up, no surprise.

"Well, not anymore." I got nothing else.

"No excuses. Meet me Friday. Six o'clock, Newark Community School of the Arts, downtown on Lincoln Park."

Nasser writes down his phone number and the address on a piece of paper, folds it up, and eases it into my pocket. That one touch sets my whole leg on fire.

I think of all the snapbacks I could say to this dude. Like, who do you think you are? With your perfect words and your pearly teeth and that old-man sweater, and what's with the fancy shoes all the time? I don't need your help with a damn thing. I'm a Diabla! But he reminded me of those two magic words: Debbie Allen. And that's enough to make me rethink my decision.

"You should smile more often, Beatriz Ayita Mendez. It's quite the vision of pulchritude." He turns to go.

The bell rings just as I'm ready to ask *pulk-uh-who*?

But Nasser Kervin Moreau is already moving through the swarm, and I'm standing in the crowd, watching him float away.

My locker combination appears in my brain like magic. When I open the door, something falls out. I bend over to pick it up. It's a Polaroid picture of me and Nasser during gym, dated September 18, 1984. The picture isn't the best quality, and whoever took it didn't get very close, but there I am standing with my nalgas hanging out of my shorts. Eyes fixed on the floor, while Nasser has his hands on my shoulders, begging me to dance.

Right beneath the picture there are words written in a language I don't recognize: Kisa ou vle.

Maricela snatches the picture out of my hand from behind before I can figure out what it means.

"Ooh, let me find out you got a novio writing you notes in . . . what is this, Swahili?"

Then here comes Julicza, grabbing the picture from Maricela. "This is definitely French. I should know 'cause I'm taking it. See, the first word means kiss. I'm not even gonna tell you what the rest of it says, 'cause it's just *nasty*!"

I snatch the picture out of Julicza's hands, but it's too late. She's already wrapping her arms around her back, gyrating her body, and making kissy sounds.

"Whatever," I snap.

"That's the new kid from the junior class? Nasa? Nassau?" Julicza finally stops cutting up.

"It's Nasser."

"Well, excuuuse me!" Maricela says.

"Guys, I don't know why this is in my locker."

It's strange because I doubt Nasser put it in there. He was walking from the opposite direction when he spotted me. Then again, he could've gotten there before I did. But how would he have gotten a picture of the two of us?

"I'm not trying to push up or nothing, but dork boy is foyne, okay? Not just fine . . . but *foyne!*" Maricela slaps fives with Julicza.

"And don't try to act like you didn't notice, Beatriz," she adds.

"He's . . . all right, I guess."

But my insides are screaming: *the boy belongs on the cover of* Essence *magazine!*

"Beatriz ain't trying to lose her focus. She's got her priorities straight, right?" Julicza adds.

I nod as air traps itself in my throat, but I give her a high five anyway.

Yes, Nasser Kervin Moreau is one tall, dark drink of agua fresca. He's smart and well-spoken and everything I am not, nor will ever be. And that is exactly why I cannot and will not even consider stepping to him.

I don't tell the girls that he invited me to take a dance class with him on Friday, when I probably should be going to the Halloween dance with my crew. I won't tell them that a part of me wants to ditch our weekly meeting, hop on the bus, and head straight downtown early to meet up with this guy. Instead, I tell myself that it's strictly business.

No one needs to know. It's just a class. One class. That just so happens to be with the cutest nerd I've ever seen at any school I've ever attended. I promise all that inside my head, knowing darn well I can lie to everyone like a master. But the one person I've never been able to lie to is myself.

Auditions to be held for "Fame"

NEWARK, New Jersey
By: Keesha Lester

Debbie Allen has taken the United States and the dance world by storm with her role as Lydia Grant in the hit film and television show "Fame." Allen first gained critical acclaim in 1980, starring in a revival of Broadway's "West Side Story" as Anita, a role that led to her first Tony Award nomination. Since then, she has won two Emmy Awards for her choreography for "Fame."

Now the producers of the show are searching for the next big star. This is your chance to audition for a role as an extra on "Fame"!

Date: Friday, November 9, 1984
Time: 7:00 p.m.
Location: Haaren High School building,
   10th Ave. & 59th St., Manhattan
What to bring: Your dancing shoes and a headshot

We hope to see some of our very own Newark talent on the small screen. As they say in show business, *break a leg*!

ACT TWO: AWAKENING

SOMETIMES ALL IT TAKES IS A SPARK,
A MEMORY,
TO CRASH INTO US,
REMIND US OF THE WHAT-IFS,
UNLEASH WHAT SIMMERS BENEATH THE DEEP,
AWAKEN THE GHOST,
AND GIVE DREAMS A SECOND CHANCE . . .

FROM: DANIEL MARTIN
TO: MIRTA MENDEZ (AND ANYONE ELSE WHO'LL LISTEN)
FOUND BY: BEATRIZ IN MAMI'S BATA POCKET WHILE DOING LAUNDRY

PRIORITIES

BY THE TIME FRIDAY COMES, I'm questioning my every move. Do I go to school? If so, I'm gonna have to see Nasser with his fancy vocabulary and those begging brownish-greenish-golden eyes. Maybe it's better if I stay and help out at the bodega. Yes, that sounds much better.

As I'm helping open up the store, Abuela asks, "¿No tienes escuela?"

"Barringer is closed for teacher workshops," I lie.

"¿Y los niños afuera con mochilas?" She gestures out the glass door.

Busted. But before I can even say anything, here comes Ms. Geraldine all off topic: "In the Philippines, education was a gift."

I about cut that woman with my eyes. The longer she hangs around Abuela, the more Spanish she's picking up. It's starting to feel like I got two old ladies all up in my business.

I finally get a word in. "Those kids go to a different school. Only Barringer is closed."

Abuela mumbles an *mm-hmm* to Ms. Geraldine, twists her lips at me, and walks away.

I spend the first couple of hours working at the counter, restocking shelves, and going outside to check on Mami. I haven't seen Mr. Martin in a bit, and judging by the look on Mami's face, I think she's been searching for him.

I grab an extra milk crate, sit next to her, and start talking to her just like I seen Mr. Martin doing. I wish I had a book of poetry or something. But all I have are my own words.

"I miss hearing your voice, Mami. Te quiero." Two words left unspoken for so long, and I don't know why. Of course I love her. But this sense of duty has taken over, robbed me of the ability to feel anything other than responsibility.

DQ, Paco, and Fredito are a few feet away from us, playing dominoes. Slamming the table, taking turns getting all riled up.

"I'm thinking about dancing again," I whisper, not wanting the others to hear.

Mami's eyes get real big, and then she grabs my hands tight. It's that same look she had when I told her I was auditioning for the pageant last year, that same look as when I started taking dance lessons once we got settled in Newark.

"Don't get too excited, Mami. I said I'm *thinking* about it."

Mami shakes her head like she don't wanna hear nothing else but a yes.

I sneakily pull out the newspaper article. As soon as she sees it, she starts to clap. She wants to talk—I can feel it—but her body says all the words that are important. She wants me to give it a try. Give myself another chance.

"¿Crees que debería ir?" I ask her.

More nods, more claps. This is the Mami I miss. If only I could hear her voice once more.

Out of nowhere, I see Rico, one of our Clinton Ave runners, round the corner of Grafton. Feet flying, huffing and puffing until he reaches DQ at the table. He bends over and whispers something in DQ's ear that ends the game immediately. DQ bolts up, darn near knocking the table to the ground.

"Yo, 911, gotta make a call," he announces.

I spring up off the milk crate, tucking the article in the pocket of Mami's bata. She rises slowly and flings open the bodega door.

"What's the emergency?" I ask, walking over to him.

"Not sure yet. I'm gonna use the pay phone and see what's up."

It turns out that someone is going around asking one too many questions. DQ tells Rico to get the word out to everyone in the crew. Missing today's meeting is not an option. Five o'clock. Don't be late. We got some nosy cats sniffing around a bit too much, and this needs to be taken care of.

But first, he's gotta make a run.

"I'll go with you," I insist.

"Maybe you should hang here."

"You're the one who said I need to be a little more Diabla and a lot less princesa, remember? Take me with you."

DQ pulls the toothpick from his lips, nods his head, and says, "That's what's up. Be back in a minute." He runs down the hill to get his car.

I head inside to grab the essentials—sneakers, Vaseline, my heavy three-finger ring. If it's gonna be a brawl, I'll be ready. Abuela catches me just as I'm geared up and about to go back outside.

She grabs my cheeks and pulls my face to her lips for a big smooch. "Princesa, mi amor. ¿Vas a bailar de nuevo?"

Mami must have shown Abuela the article. Dios mio. A pain stabs right through me. I have bigger problems right now.

"I'm not sure, Abuela. I'll try my best."

Abuela squeezes my arms like she's trying to shake some good sense into me. "Ahora escúchame bien. Today, Mirta's happy. You should dance for youself, pero hazlo por ella también."

Truth is, this is something I want to do . . . but I made a promise.

"Sí, Abuela, I'll go." I tell her and myself, and this time it doesn't feel like a complete lie.

DQ drives me, Fredito, and Paco down to the South Ward. Bass thumping, Run-D.M.C. blasting. I'm in the back seat, the pace of my heart in rhythm with the beat, my palms growing clammy. I glance over and look at Paco. He spits in a washcloth, pulls a Glock from his boot, and starts shining it like it's a pair of penny loafers.

"Junito never showed you this side of Diablo life." Paco's top lip rises while the rest of his face remains still.

DQ lowers the music a bit. "Oh, don't you worry. Beatriz is all in now, right? We might as well start calling her *Junita*." I notice DQ's eyes squinted at me through the rearview mirror.

"All in." I give him a hard stare back. "Pa' siempre."

We pull up to the alley behind RL Liquors, and the second we see Miguel it's pretty obvious what happened. He was approached by someone asking questions. Judging by the chichón bulging above his eye, I'm guessing that person didn't like what Miguel had to say. Still, he honored the code. No talking about connects, even if it leads to getting a beatdown.

"Yo, DQ, I ain't said a word." Miguel is trying to look as tough as possible. But that's hard to do when you got a mountain growing on your face. I know all about it.

"What'd they wanna know?" Fredo's in Miguel's face now.

"Who's running the Diablos, you?" Miguel's breathing speeds up.

"What did they look like?" DQ asks.

"Some kind of accent, maybe Jamaican. Brown skin. She was a little darker than you, Beatriz."

"She? Wait, it was some chick?" DQ folds over and laughs.

Miguel won't even look at us.

Then Paco adds in more fire. "Yo, you let a girl house you?"

"It wasn't like that at first! She was all batting her eyelashes and junk. She caught me off guard and then drove off." Miguel is falling all over himself to explain.

"What kind of car?" I ask.

My pulse starts to skip before he answers.

"I don't know. Maybe a Pontiac or Trans Am," Miguel says.

Terror rises up in me. Maybe in DQ too, 'cause the way he's looking at me says so. He was there that day. For the first part of the drive-by.

Say something, Beatriz. Tell him what happened in the

empty lot. The threat that guy said. The chick with the dreads. The words do a slow crawl up my throat, morph into an image of homeboy sending somebody to come back to carry out his promise. That right there kills all the words I planned to say.

DQ arranges for Miguel to lay low somewhere for the next couple of days. Even if it was a girl, he says he can't be too sure that she's not working for someone else. In the meantime, he doubles up our runners on each corner, and we speed back to Broadway to hold our meeting.

Everyone shows up on time, many of them dressed in costumes for the Barringer Halloween dance.

"I can't believe you're not going," Julicza says to me as she walks to an empty seat.

I don't respond. I'm too busy looking at the clock, and each move of the second hand hits me with too many thoughts. Like how I should keep my behind home and do what I do best: protect my family. But also how bad I want to go. Hop the bus downtown, walk through the doors of the dance studio, breathe in the rhythms and dreams I've almost forgotten about. Breathe out the fear, the emptiness, the hope for something I might never have again.

Everyone drops their cash on the table. No leftovers, no shortages. Even Juan is on point today. The money piles higher and higher in perfect neat stacks.

Everyone is talking over each other as they sit down. DQ bangs the mallet against the table to get the meeting started.

"It appears we may have some people out there asking about the Diablos again," he begins.

"Five-o?" Julicza calls out.

"Maybe undercover, maybe not." That revelation starts a low rumble.

DQ says one thing is clear: we gotta start running a tighter operation. It's time to do away with wearing full colors, at least for now. Only one red item of clothing is allowed. Nothing more. And we gotta be more careful with delivering product to our customers. Be more discreet. Not out in the open. Stick to alleyways and abandoned buildings. Even better, anywhere behind closed doors.

"And in the meantime, I think I'll have some of the crew in lockup teach the Macoutes a lesson about what happens when you try to step to the Diablos." DQ looks straight at me, his words singing like a poem in my head. But a tiny voice whispers back: *Is that really what you want?*

Ricky Gonzalez, runner from the Central Ward, calls out, "And if they come after our territory again?"

DQ runs his fingertips across his thick goatee. "Well, their aim better be immaculate, because this time I won't miss."

Everybody starts snapping after that.

"I'm gonna call it a wrap for tonight, everyone." DQ looks at his watch.

It's almost five forty-five. Dance class starts in fifteen minutes and it takes twenty-five minutes to get downtown.

Everyone collects their share from Paco and leaves out the back exit, just as quietly as they entered. DQ is the only one who stays behind. He starts walking around, cleaning up.

"You know what, DQ, I'm good. I can handle this."

I speed walk through the room, collecting used cups and napkins.

"What's the hurry all about, princesa? You act like you got a hot date or something."

I don't need a mirror to see the red surfacing on my cheeks. DQ stops cleaning and leans straight into my face.

"Beatriz Mendez, ¿tienes novio? Don't make me have to give somebody a beatdown."

"I don't have a boyfriend." It's the truth.

For a second I consider telling him about the dance class. That I have a chance to audition for *Fame*, but first I need to practice a little. Actually a lot. But what if DQ thinks that wanting to dance makes me look weak? Especially with everything going on right now? What if he thinks I'm losing my focus? And that's technically not the truth. My job is to take care of Mami and keep my promise to Junito. Everything else—dancing and novios—isn't as important.

"I was thinking about something you said during the meeting," I say.

"Oh yeah, what's that?" DQ throws a few plastic cups in the garbage.

"I'm not sure about the hit. At least not now. Can we wait a little longer?"

Paco peeks his bearded face through the back door, looks at DQ and points his nose up. "Let's roll," he says.

DQ smiles and immediately stops playing house-keeper. "We'll talk about that later. I gotta run."

"Oh, why the rush, DQ? Got a hot pre-birthday date?" Now I'm up in his business.

"Something like that, but hey, I'm turning nineteen

this weekend. So I'm a grown man. You, Beatriz, have a long time to go before you're allowed to date. I'll let you when you turn thirty."

"Oh, *let me*, huh?" Sometimes the pain of missing my brother hurts so bad, but it's still nice to have DQ around.

"Stay safe, Beatriz."

"Happy early birthday, DQ."

And then he slips through the door.

I wait a good five minutes, though the passing of each second causes my anxiety to go through the roof. When I think I've given DQ and everyone else enough time to be gone, I stuff a big wad of cash in my pocket. The second I do, I'm having a Beatriz versus Beatriz argument in my head.

Me: What are you bringing money to the dance school for, Beatriz?

Also me: Ain't no fighting it. You know exactly why.

I gather up what I remember I'll need for class: a small towel, bottle of water, and my old dance shoes. As for the blade in my cheek? Yeah, that's gotta go. I slide it in its holder and place it in my jacket pocket. Then I head outside and make my way toward the bus stop. Broadway is alive tonight with the excitement and mystery of Halloween. Folks walk around dressed in costumes of all kinds—an angel, two Cabbage Patch Kids, a crew of Ghostbusters, and up ahead, a devil . . . I think. Red cape, brown bodysuit, red horns, and over the face, a random hockey mask, like in those Jason movies. Looks like somebody didn't think their costume all the way through. The hockey-devil bumps right into me as we pass each other.

"Watch it," the person whispers, not stopping to look me in the eye.

"No, you watch it!" I whip myself around, but the devil is already gone.

FIRST TO DANCE

BY THE TIME THE BUS pulls up and stops around the block from the Newark Community School of the Arts, I'm already more than a half hour late.

The music hits me before I even get to the door. I feel it vibrating against the sidewalk. For a moment I hesitate and ask myself what the hell I'm doing here.

Through the glass windows, I see Nasser standing among the rows and rows of dancers, dressed in the type of clothes that make him look like he's serious about his art. White tank top showing off muscles I didn't know he had. Black dance pants, loose where they should be and tight where it matters most. And here I am in my baggy sweatshirt, stirrup pants, and red Reeboks. My hair is at least five inches too long, begging to be cut, combed, relaxed—something.

In the corner, a drummer beats his drum. In the center of the floor, a dance teacher twirls like there's no tomorrow. Even the tips of her fingers have perfect rhythm. She's short like me, but you wouldn't know it from the way she's moving, like her legs could touch the sky if she tried.

I can't go in there. What was I thinking? Just as I get ready to turn and head straight back to the bus stop, Nasser catches sight of me standing outside the glass door. He runs outside.

"Glad you made it. I was starting to think you weren't coming. You're gonna love it. Señorita Amaro is amazing!" He's got starlight gleaming in his eyes.

I chew on my bottom lip and try to come up with my best excuse. *I'm not prepared. I'll look wack like that. Everybody else clearly knows what they're doing.*

"Look, I can't stay. I got a lot going on back home. I just came to tell you that."

Nasser doesn't care. He just grabs me by the wrist and pulls me inside.

The teacher sees me and cuts off the music. "Why, hello there . . . you're *late*."

Rows and rows of dancers dart their eyes at me, hawking me up and down, probably wondering why I even bothered to come, since class is basically over. No worries, 'cause I'm thinking the same thing.

"On your feet! Miguelito, from the top!" Señorita Amaro screams.

The drummer attacks the drum like a fire is burning inside of him.

"Try and keep up." She cuts her eyes at me and yells, "A five, six, seven, eight!"

The class begins the routine. Yeah, the one I would have learned had I showed up on time. They're kicking and jumping and spinning and soaring through the roof. And there I am, mimicking every other move, wishing I could spin the earth backward. They go left, I go right; they go up, I go down. The awkwardness of how rusty I am hangs in the space between me and Señorita Amaro, and all the while I catch her looking at me—too much.

She throws her hand in the air, a signal to cut the music. "Good work today, everyone. Same time next week! Class is dismissed."

And just like that my whole world crashes. The room empties out, and I'm ready to follow right behind everyone as they exit. But Nasser won't hear of it. He makes me stand right alongside him.

He waits for the teacher to come over. "This is the girl I was telling you about, Señorita Amaro."

I stand there, begging my body not to burst out into a cold sweat.

"Nasser tells me you dance. That it's in your blood—in your name, even," she says.

"I used to dance. . . . I took classes for a while at Maria Priadka's. . . . And my mom taught me the dances of Puerto Rico. Almost competed in a pageant once . . . but it didn't work out."

Every word is dressed in fear. I want to escape. I want to stay. I want to run. I want to feel that music again and get it right this time.

"Well, that's too bad. I think the pageant world could use some spicing up with a good dancer. So you like competitions, huh?" She takes a sip from her bottle of water.

"I haven't danced in a long time."

"What happened?"

I hesitate before speaking. "One day I just lost the music is all."

"Well, we just have to help you find it again. Miguelito!" Señorita Amaro sticks her thumb and index finger in her mouth and whistles loudly. "¡Música, por favor!"

Next thing I know, the drummer starts to play a beat, a different one this time. Slow at first, then climbing and climbing to a pace that my heart can barely keep up with.

"You feel that? That's the rhythm of Africa. Spain wasn't your motherland. Africa was." She points to Nasser. "And yours." She points to me. "And mine. It's where we come from. We are no different, you and I. Haiti, Puerto Rico, Cuba . . . one people connected to Africa, our motherland."

Haiti? Nasser is from Haiti?

I don't have time to ask because Miguelito is pounding the timbales now. I feel a tingle in my toes. It begs the rest of my body to move, but I fight the urge. I don't want to be here. I tell myself that over and over again. This is not where I belong. But then that beat sinks in so deep, I forget I have knees. By this point, Nasser is flailing his arms and kicking his feet. And it looks like he is kicking away whatever pain he's got locked up inside him too. My back arches, my hands take flight, and it's like I'm flying through the roof.

The rhythm quickens. Lion. Tiger. I am a hunter searching for its next meal. All three of us are moving, releasing, connecting to the rhythm that bleeds from Miguelito's fingers to the skin of the timbales. Nasser clasps his hands into mine, and Señorita Amaro takes a step back. Together we soar. My hands lock in his, like everything and nothing at the same time. He spins me round the globe, and my legs flick straight and back with precision.

When Miguelito taps out a final *pam pam*, my body goes limp, and I collapse to the floor.

Señorita Amaro claps wildly. "Now *that's* what I'm talking 'bout!"

But Nasser is scared out of his mind. "Beatriz, are you okay? Say something." His hands graze my sweaty face.

"She's fine, Nasser. I know exactly what she's feeling. When you're a true dancer here in the corazón"—she points to her heart—"you can't escape it. And when you ignore that desire, that passion, even for a day, it can exhaust you once you finally revisit it."

Nasser helps me stand on my two feet. Señorita Amaro walks to the far end of the studio to chat with some of the other staff members. We're putting our regular shoes on when she walks back over to us.

"You two make a nice couple," Señorita Amaro says.

Nasser and I look at each other and smile weakly.

"He's not my—"

Señorita Amaro cuts me off. "Well, I don't mean in that way! I mean the dancing. The chemistry. I saw a fire in both of you tonight. Now Beatriz, you need some more work, though, on your feet and hand positioning, especially if you're auditioning for *Fame*."

"I know." I chew on my bottom lip.

"Of course, we can get you some proper training. Two weeks isn't enough time, but we can at least straighten out your lines, work on your form in time for the big day."

"But I'm not a student—"

"Yet," Nasser jumps in. "She's registering for classes . . . *today*."

"I am?" I cough the words out, but I'm no idiota.

Nasser purses his lips and gives me a shut-yo-mouth-and-play-along look. And on the inside, half of me is screaming at the other half. *You knew exactly what you were doing when you packed your stash.*

Okay, I guess I'm enrolling in dance classes. Money ain't the issue. Time is. I don't have time to dance, be in a gang, and take care of Mami.

Señorita Amaro hands me the paperwork with the requirements and fees, which I fill out before pulling out a wad of cash and forking over the tuition like it's nothing.

Both she and Nasser look at me with the same question painted on their faces: *Where the heck did you get all that money?*

"Oh, this?" I point to it and quickly start up my lie. "I work at my mom's bodega and today was payday."

Señorita Amaro puckers her lips, almost like Abuela does, and throws in a stern, "See you next week . . . *on time*."

It's almost nine o'clock when we leave the dance studio. Buses are running less often by then.

"I can drive you home," Nasser says.

It is a little cold. And I'm exhausted as all get-out. Maybe I can take just this one ride. "Okay, cool."

We walk to his car, and I realize it's not a car. It's a yellow taxi. "Umm, Nasser?"

"Yeah, I know. I'll tell you all about it. Hop in."

Nasser revs up the engine and pulls off under a full moon. I'm not sure why, but when he asks me for directions,

I give him all the wrong ones that take us the extra-long way. I have him drive me all through Branch Brook Park. The trees are especially pretty in the moonlight. His super-white teeth gleam as he smiles while talking.

"You sure you live in Newark?" Nasser asks. "Because I don't think it takes forty minutes to get around the city . . . not that I'm complaining or anything."

I just smile at him, and then he turns up the music on the radio. New Edition's "Cool It Now" comes on.

"What's your story, Beatriz?"

"I don't have one," I respond.

"Everyone has a story."

"Okay, so then tell me yours, Mr. Taxi Man."

Nasser Moreau speaks three languages—English, French, and Creole (and is learning Spanish)—and is damn near perfect at math and dancing and reading and basically breathing. But he doesn't actually say that last part. I already knew that from watching him at school.

"My parents left Léogâne in Haiti to come to the States so my sister and I could make something of ourselves. The taxi belongs to my dad, and my mom is a home health aide. They bust their butts so I can have a shot at this thing called the American dream."

"Why didn't you tell me you're Haitian?" I scan his face, not really sure what I'm looking for. Something familiar? But I come up empty.

Out of nowhere a cat bolts across the street, making him swerve the car a bit. It distracts him, I guess, because he never answers my question. So I try another one.

"When did you say you moved to Newark?" I ask.

"I finished out my sophomore year in Miami, and then we came here over the summer."

So he wasn't here in April. Could he still be connected to the Macoutes somehow?

"I didn't realize that introducing myself as Haitian was a necessity around these parts. Where'd you think I was from? Don't tell me—"

"Jamaica," I blurt. Laughter spills out of his mouth like a rushing waterfall.

"And let me guess the other one: Africa?"

I nod shyly and feel like my intelligence level lowers five points.

"That's like saying Puerto Ricans and Dominicans are the same."

"Two different places, idiota!" I slap Nasser one good time on the shoulder.

"Bingo!"

Ahead the light turns yellow, and he slows the car and stops by the time the red light appears. He turns his face to mine, the rows of street lamps glittering in the darkness of his eyes.

"Is it a problem that I'm Haitian?" he asks.

I try to stop the oversize lump lodging itself in my throat. Try to block out the words I'd heard Abuela say over and over back in Aguadilla: mejora la raza. Translation: Don't even think about getting with someone with dark skin. Life is hard enough when you're dark. So why make it harder? I never understood that backward thinking, especially since Abuela is dark herself.

"No, I don't care where you're from. Far as I'm concerned, you're my Caribbean brother." I hold my hand up for a high five, and Nasser's smile spans the perimeter of his whole head.

I change the convo real quick. "So what you wanna do, like after you leave Barringer?"

"That's the problem. There's so much I want to do. I thought about being a lawyer because I love history—"

"And words," I add.

He starts laughing. "Yeah, that too! I like the arts—dancing, poetry, singing, guitar. And I already told you how I go to town in the kitchen."

"What's your specialty?"

"Oh, I make rice and beans like you wouldn't believe!" He grins and those teeth gleam.

"And what do you sing?"

"Anything."

"Then sing a song for me."

He shakes his head, puts the signal on, and turns onto Broadway. As we draw closer to home, I know my time is almost up. I point to Grafton Ave and ask him to turn there because I know for a fact that if any of the guys are standing in front of the bodega, this scene won't play out too well. I can just picture it now, the Diablos threatening Nasser to stay away from me, even though there's nothing going on between the two of us. I think.

"One day I will sing a song for you, Beatriz Ayita Mendez." The smile in Nasser's eyes glows.

We sit parked in the taxi at the bottom of the hill near the train tracks. Random people knocking on the window asking for rides. He turns every one of them down. The saxophone intro for "Caribbean Queen" rolls in through the radio speakers.

I'm sitting there trying to think of what to say next. *Err, see you at school. Umm, thanks for the ride.*

But all I can do is stare at the halo of moonlight that frames his face. Julicza and Maricela were right. Damn, this boy is fine. Make that *foyne*.

The memory of us standing at my locker comes flooding back. Him saying I was a vision of pulchritude, which, it turns out, is derived from Latin, meaning "beautiful." *Thank you, Merriam-Webster dictionary!*

But I also remember him floating away and what happened when I opened my locker.

"Hey, I've been meaning to show you something." I pull out the Polaroid picture from my bag.

Nasser turns on the light in the car to get a better look. "Whoa! Who took this photo?" He looks at me, puzzled.

"I think I'm the one who should be asking you that. My friends think maybe it's for the yearbook or something."

He shrugs his shoulders.

"Any idea what it says? You're the one with the international vocabulary."

"Kisa ou vle. It's written in my native language, Haitian Creole. It says 'what you want.'" Nasser's voice rises above Billy Ocean's soulful melody.

"What I want? You mean, like, what *do* I want?"

"No, this is a declarative, not an interrogative," he explains.

"You're killing me, bro."

"The words are telling you *this is what you want*. And judging by the picture, I'm guessing whoever wrote it is trying to say you want . . . me?" His voice turns soft.

I snatch the picture out of his hand. Why is this note

written in Creole, Nasser's language—the same language of the Macoutes?

"But I don't want you." And as soon as I say that, my shoulders cave in. "What I mean to say is, I don't want anything."

Except for my life and my mom and my brother back.

"Whoever took the picture must think I like you or something," I blurt out.

Nasser's mouth spreads wider than the Passaic River behind the projects. "Well . . . do you?"

If there was a way to disappear into thin air, now would be the time.

"You're different, Beatriz."

"How so?"

"I can't put my finger on it, but I just know you're not like any girl I've ever met. For starters, you're not one of those wannabe gangsta girls starting drama—"

The ball growing in my throat feels too big, too unmanageable.

"And your face . . ." His voice drifts off.

I pull my hair forward to cover what others say is no longer there, though to me, it remains as clear as the day it was bashed in.

"It's unique. Like a piece of art."

You mean the abstract kind, where colors and lines are thrown together and nothing makes sense?

"I, um, had an accident a few months ago. Before that, my face was different . . . better." And that's all I'm sharing.

"Well, I'm glad I met you with the face you have now." He smiles, and I swear I want to hear him say that a hundred more times.

"So about me and you?" Nasser leans in a little closer to my shoulder.

I peep those eyes, that neck, that chin once more, looking for a reason to run away. There's no tattoos, no battle scars, not a single thing that screams, "I'm in a gang."

I know what's coming next. *Please don't ask me out. Please don't ask me out.* But this little voice inside says, *Please do.*

"Are we going to audition for *Fame* or what? Those casting directors won't know what hit them."

My belly becomes a pit of relief and disappointment. "Yeah. Audition. Um, sure, but let me talk it over with my mom first."

"Do you think your father will be okay with this? I can talk to him if you'd like, so he won't be perturbed."

"My dad is back in Puerto Rico."

Saying those words reminds me that he is anywhere but here. And in that moment the memory of his face appears. A reminder of what love and hate looks like, all wrapped in one.

"Oh. Well, now you have to audition and make it in, so he can see you on TV!" Nasser's all hyped up again.

My skin turns hot, and suddenly I'm ready to go. What if I do make it on *Fame* and Papi sees? Will he come running back, apologize, and make everything right? And as for Nasser, can I even trust this guy? I mean he's nice and all, but everybody's got a hidden side.

"I'll let you know. But right now, I gotta go." I slam the door behind me and pretend I live in the projects, walking farther down the hill, past the train tracks. The last thing I need is for him to see me at the bodega surrounded by a bunch of Diablos. Especially if it turns out that he's a Macoute after all.

Track Three: Dance the Cha Cha, 1977
Tonight's dream starts with boobs.

I am pressed against the softness of Mami's chest. Mami tiptoes past Papi snoring on the floor, Junito glued to her side, as she gently closes the casita door. I hear the rhythmic crunch of coconut leaves beneath Mami's feet—and the call of the coquí in the distance.

"¿A dónde vamos, Mami?" Junito whispers through the darkness.

The soft hum of a car engine sounds off in the distance, and the car flashes its lights to make itself known. Mami speeds her footsteps at the sight. The faster she moves, the more I become aware of my surroundings: the way the frogs sing ko keee!, *the stars glittering the sky, the sound of salsa swelling in the barrio.*

Mami kisses my forehead before answering Junito. "Todo va estar bien, mi'jo. This will be over soon."

Tío Luis, Mami's brother, steps out of the car to help Mami put us and the bags in.

Junito and I sit in the back of Tío Luis's Toyota. It's the same car Tío drives to pick me, Junito, and all my cousins up on Thursdays to go to the playa and buy us limber de coco. We always devour our frozen treats, coconut juice dripping down our chins, feet sinking in the sand. We dance, sing, and play in the ocean until the sun kisses the sky good night.

"Now remember what I told you," Tío whispers, not realizing I am awake.

"Tía Inez's friend Lucy will have her husband, Ronaldo, pick us up at Newark Airport, yes?" Mami replies.

Newark? Is that a town in Puerto Rico? *Junito gently squeezes my hand. The moonlight pours in through our back windows, shining a spotlight on his mouth. That last fight at the arena left him with an extra lip.*

"Exáctamente. Ronaldo speaks Portuguese, but it's close enough to Spanish. You should be fine. He will take you to their apartment. They already have a spare room set up for you and the kids. It's not much, but you will be comfortable."

"¿Y no tengo que pagar nada? Are you sure?" Mami sounds scared.

"Lucy is family. She won't charge you a penny. Inez took her in when Lucy's mother died. She took care of her until she got on her feet. That's when she met Ronaldo and married him. Lucy is more than happy to return the favor. Just use the money our mother gave you to get you and the kids started." Tío Luis is patient.

A tear crawls out from Mami's swollen eye.

Tío grabs her hand and presses it to his chest. "Te lo prometo, hermana. They will help you find a job. Lucy works at a hotel and her husband works at some department store called Bamberger's. They'll help you get the kids into school. You'll be on your own before you know it."

"What if the schools don't let them in? It's already December. Luis, nosotros no hablamos bien el inglés. What if I can't find a job? What if the kids fail?"

Now Mami is really crying. "You gotta turn back," she tells Tío Luis. "This is going to break his heart. And Beatriz!

You know how much she loves her papi. Voy a hablar con él, Luis. I can get him to stop drinking and stop—"

"Hitting you? ¿Y Junito? And meanwhile Beatriz sees all this every day como si fuera normal? That's what you call love? Is that what you want for your children? To let them grow up thinking it's okay to let your husband beat you?" There is anger in Tío's voice. It's deep, and it's enough to make Mami stop talking.

By the time we get to the airport, it's almost four in the morning. Tío parks the car at the terminal, and Junito and I immediately pretend we're sleeping when he turns around to check on us.

"Remember who you're doing this for. Todo por ellos." I can tell he's pointing straight at us.

"He'll come knocking on your door the second the rooster crows," Mami warns.

Tío slaps one fist in the other hand. "Lo espero."

Mami gets us up while Tío pulls our belongings out of the trunk of his car. Three bags, one for each of us. That is all we leave with that night. Three bags, lots of tears, and an endless supply of island memories.

The pain of it all swirls inside my head and jolts me awake. My eyes scan the darkness, confused, trying to forget the life that once was, wishing for a different life that could've been.

MAKING THE CALL

"DO YOU HAVE THE VALUE of the variable, Ms. Mendez?" I smell Mr. Hankerson's breath even before he gets up next to me. A disastrous mix of wet dog, sweaty locker room, and a pinch of caca.

I sit up in my seat, and the whole class turns around to look at me. This right here is why I hate school.

"I'm not sure I heard the question," I say.

"One more time. What is the value of n in the following equation: $4 + n = -5 + (-9)$?"

I want to understand him, but this man is speaking Russian or something.

"Yo, this is *wack*!" Julicza blurts out, and the whole class starts dying laughing. The bell rings, thank God, but as everybody darts out the door, Mr. Dragonbreath tells me to stay behind.

I can see that Julicza and Maricela are waiting for me in the hall.

Mr. Hankerson walks over to his desk and pulls out a

folder with my name on it. "You know, Beatriz, Mrs. Ruiz from the guidance department came around here asking about your grades and how you're doing, and this is what I had to show her."

He whips the folder open with copies of my tests, decorated in red Ds and Fs.

"I'm gonna start studying more," I say quickly.

"We're already at the end of October and the marking period will be over before you know it. You rarely come to class, and when you do, I'm not getting much out of you. Don't you want better for yourself?"

That seems to be the question of the year. I did, once upon a time. But I say, "I do want better."

"I'd like to recommend a peer tutor for you. She's a senior, new to the school, a real math wizard. You can sign up in the guidance department. Here is her name." Mr. Hankerson pulls an index card from the drawer and writes down "Amy Marcel."

I remember Mrs. Ruiz saying something about a peer tutor a while back. I've been glad she'd forgotten about it. But I guess I wasn't escaping after all.

"Do you know her?" he asks.

"Um, no." There's a sapo concho in my throat. "I don't. You know Barringer's such a big school and all. And like you said, she's a senior."

Straight up, that name sounds like a white girl. I'm already rolling my eyes. The last thing I need is some chick, especially some blanquita, thinking she's better than me. But I don't say any of that because I know where that card is going. Straight to the basura.

"What about a different tutor?" I blurt out.

"Ohhh?" Mr. Hankerson draws out the word until the fumes almost burn me to ash. "Who'd you have in mind?"

"Do you know anything about Nasser Moreau?" *Like, is he a gangsta dressed in a dork disguise?*

"Ah, very smart kid. Stays to himself and out of trouble, which"—Mr. Hankerson darts his eyes to Julicza in the hall—"I find refreshing."

I don't know why, but something about hearing Mr. Hankerson say that brings up memories of our night together at dance class and on the ride home. The tension in my neck loosens up.

"Is he on the tutor list?" I ask.

"No, and even though I think you two would be a good study match . . ."

That ain't all he'd be good for.

"I'm going to require that you be paired with Amy. She is in my AP class. Nasser just enrolled in my honors class and is a year behind Amy. Tutoring will take place after school in the library. Amy will be there with the other volunteers. I had her matched up with a sophomore, but I think you'll be a better pairing. I'll have to make a note of the switch. Anyway, sessions begin tomorrow after school in the library." Mr. Hankerson hands me a schedule.

As soon as it hits my hands, my eyes stank-roll on their own.

"Ms. Mendez, this is not up for debate. I can't pass you at this rate. And judging from your grades, none of your other teachers can either. Aren't you a native Spanish speaker?" Mr. Hankerson asks.

"Yeah, and?"

"Then there's no reason why you should be failing that

too. Listen, I can tell that you're a smart young lady. But unless you do something soon, I can't see you passing. And then you would have to attend summer school."

Part of me wants to tell off this dude with his funky-behind breath. I'm not trying to be stuck in no hot school in the summer. I don't care how good sales are up in here. So I just nod my head and reluctantly promise that I'll show up to tutoring.

The late bell rings. Maricela and Julicza stick their heads in the door, and Julicza starts making stupid dragon-roar sounds.

"I'll write you a late pass for your next class, but not for your friends." Mr. Hankerson darts his eyes at my girls. "You might want to be careful of the company you keep, particularly Ms. Feliciano."

Julicza and Mr. Hankerson have had this hate-hate relationship brewing since the first day of school.

I thank Mr. Hankerson for the pass and join my girls in the hallway. As soon as we start walking, I see Nasser and some other dude going the opposite way. Two peas in a pod. Dressed like teachers, walking like they got steel rods rammed up their backs. At least he finally found a friend. I don't hear their full conversation, but I can tell they're discussing something that sounds *intelligent*. And in that moment all I see is our differences—my inner darkness to his outer light, my yin to his yang. His one lonely dork friend to my gang. We'll never be alike.

Nasser catches sight of me and says hi, but I refuse to look at him or speak.

"I think dork boy has a thing for you," Maricela says.

"Sure does," Julicza chimes in.

We get to home economics just as the teacher, Mrs. Ross, is yelling at folks to pull out their notebooks.

I stop the girls at the door before going in. "Look, I was thinking we should cancel the meeting on Friday," I announce.

Julicza twists her face. "Um, what you mean by *we*? We are not in charge, nena."

"It's just that I got a lot going on Friday. Inventory for the bodega . . ." I think of some more lies. "And repairs in the basement. Can't have the meeting down there."

Maricela shrugs and says, "I'm always down for a day off." She walks into class.

Meanwhile, Julicza stands with her arms locked in a who-do-you-think-you-are position.

"You already know DQ ain't canceling. He'll just move the location. Business stops for no one. What's up with you?" she asks.

"Nothing." I head in to home ec, keeping my thoughts and my business trapped between my lips.

FIGURING IT OUT

AFTER SCHOOL, WHEN I get to the bodega, Mami sees
me, rushes my way, and hugs me like she hasn't seen me
in years. I let her hold me tight, wait for her to speak,
mumble, whisper. I'll take anything. I get nothing but a
blank stare and a gust of cold air biting at my cheeks.

"Mami, you're gonna have to cut back on sitting outside
all day."

She nods slowly, jawbone clenched beneath her skin.

"I danced my heart out last week at that class, Mami. I
haven't felt that alive in so long."

She presses her hands together, like a prayer. She's asking me to dance.

"Right here? In the street?"

More nods, slight smile. I look around to make sure no
one is looking. Broadway is one big hustle, with moving cars
and feet up and down the street. No one is paying attention
to me, so I give it a try.

Hands up, shoulders back, back straight, neck tilted, feet

in third position, just like Señorita Amaro does it. I tap out the rhythms drifting up and down my 'hood. Two steps left, *cha cha*, hands clap as the traffic light flashes green-yellow-red, *one, two, three*. Knees bent in demi-plié, swaying lightly like the wind bending branches. My invisible partner rocks me forward, leans me into an imaginary dip, and then I take a bow.

Mami claps uncontrollably, and in that moment I want the whole world around us to disappear.

"I can't wait to go back on Friday," I say as I take a seat on the empty milk crate next to her. That's when I notice the sun pouring its rays into the center of Mami's empty eyes.

"Mr. Martin hasn't been coming around as much, huh?"

Slight nod, weak smile. The wind picks up, and Mami tightens the shawl around her shoulders.

"I have a new friend too. There's this boy . . . his name is Nasser. He takes dance class with me." I look at the ground, searching for what to reveal next.

The picture I found in my locker? The fact that I might be falling for a Haitian boy? Even though everything about it feels like a betrayal to Junito.

DQ pulls up in his car with Paco and Fredito just as I'm bringing Mami inside from the cold.

"Yo, Beatriz, I gotta talk to you," DQ calls out the window.

Translation? Meet him in the basement in five.

I get Mami settled upstairs before heading downstairs and cracking the back door open. DQ and the guys slip in quietly.

"What up? We can't stay here long. . . ." I set up my lie. "The repairs aren't done yet, so it's not safe."

"This room don't look no different to me." Fredito adds his two cents though nobody asked him to.

DQ scans the space and then runs his tongue across his teeth. "I just wanted to let you know it's handled."

"What's handled?" I ask.

"No more interrogations. We ain't had another incident since Miguel. Time is up for the Macoutes and Clemenceau 'Soukie' Mondesir. Who the hell names their kid that anyway? That's just asking for a lifetime of ass whoopings!"

That sends the guys into roaring laughter. My heart becomes dead weight and falls to the floor.

"You did what?" My voice scares me.

"Oh, it hasn't happened yet, but it's set up. Good things take time, princesa."

Hate is marinating inside me. That voice rises up in my head. *New pop blay! You talk, we'll be back!*

Say something, Beatriz! "You can't go through with it! Call it off!"

It's the best I got.

"¡Cálmate!" DQ is all smiles. "I got this, and I got you."

DQ places his hands on my shoulders to make me sit. "Here, look at this new product from our connect in New York. It's called Sour Diesel. This, plus cocaine, will make us more money than ever before. Pretty dope, right?"

Paco pulls his jacket off, unzips a pocket, and flips it over. Nickel and dime bags of reefer spill across the table. I don't want them here.

"I thought you would tell me before you ordered a hit, out of respect for Junito," I say.

DQ pulls his face in close. "Just like you kept me in the loop when you thought you'd try to cancel this week's meeting?"

I lean backward, leaving a space between us. "I wasn't trying to run things, DQ. I just got a lot going on here."

The heat of his breath makes its way toward my skin. "We sell all of this, and it's gonna be a big payday for you, for me, for all of us. Can't have nothing stopping our progress. And next time, before you think about changing things, talk to me first."

"You're not my brother." The words come out like a flame.

I'm not even sure who I am right now. But I feel like running. Grabbing Mami and Abuela, a suitcase for each of us, and hopping on the next plane back to Aguadilla. Better yet, one of those countries with the fancy words Nasser always talks about. This isn't what I ever wanted.

"Listen, you're gonna have to get with it. This is the life of a Diablo. We sell drugs to survive. Bills get paid off the backs of other people's addictions. And that's not our problem."

But what if I don't want to do this anymore? The thought sinks deep in my heart but never makes its way out of my mouth.

"You still in this, right? Don't tell me you backing out. 'Cause you and I both know how that turns out." DQ crosses his arms and stares at me.

I wanna tell him I'm done. But what are the consequences? When Junito first started the gang, the rules were clear: blood in, blood out. To be a Diablo, you had to get jumped in. I remember mine like it was yesterday. Twelve years old. Right by the train tracks, far away from Mami's protective eyes. Me versus Junito's fake girlfriend. Nixida Vigo had me by three years and at least six inches. Kicked my ass something good too. Never laid a hand on my face, though. Junito's request, of course.

I survived being jumped in. But what would "blood out" look like if I wanted to leave? I decide right then and there that I can't tell DQ nothing—not about dancing, not about Nasser, and definitely not about the picture in my locker. At least until I've bought some time to figure things out on my own.

BEATRIZ VS. THE HUMAN TURTLE

THE SCHOOL LIBRARY is bustling when I show up for tutoring the next day. If I didn't know any better, I'd think it's a hangout spot up in here. Each table is filled with students—talking, low-key rapping, doing everything but what they actually came here for. From the looks of it, Mrs. Ruiz and the librarian, Mrs. Arcentales, don't have an ounce of control.

"I'm so glad you could make it, Beatriz. You're doing the right thing." Mrs. Ruiz flips a page on her clipboard and checks my name off the list.

"Yeah, well, Mr. Hankerson didn't really give me a choice," I admit.

Sometimes I put on a front, like this whole school thing ain't for me, but deep down I *do* want to do better. For me. For Mami too. And maybe making better grades is a start.

"Sign your name on this sheet. Amy is the girl over there. New student, don't know much about her, but her grades are off the charts. You're in good hands."

Tucked in the back corner, there's a brown-skinned girl at a table with half her face buried in a book, sitting alone.

"Cool. Thanks, Mrs. Ruiz."

Amy spots me before I reach the table. All of a sudden she starts pulling at her hair—a short layered bob that touches the tops of her ears. Was she expecting some hot guy to show up?

"Yo, what's up? I'm Beatriz."

She doesn't respond. Instead she tugs at her turtleneck and pulls it up until it almost covers her nose, literally transforming herself into a human turtle.

What's with this chick? I mean, damn, do I stink? I lower my chin and do a quick pit sniff. After all, I did have gym today. Nope—still fresh.

"Mr. Hankerson told me I was tutoring some sophomore named Kareem." She finally speaks, checking her log sheet.

I fall into the chair across from her.

"Um, sorry to disappoint you." I shrug my shoulders.

Just then, Nasser walks into the library. Earlier, I ran into him on the way to the cafeteria. When I told him I was signed up for tutoring, he got all huffy-puffy about it, bragging how nobody would be a better tutor for me than him and how he's gonna crash my session. I told that boy to not come looking for me after school—or ever for that matter. His middle name should be Hardheaded instead of Kervin.

"Well, what do you need help with? We could start with operations and variables," Amy says.

I hear her, but then again I don't. Because Nasser has made his way to a shelf a few feet behind Amy. He pulls out that big-ass etymology book from his backpack and is now staring at me. With those eyes. Dark and light and every-thing in between. Hypnotizing me when I'm supposed to be getting my study on. Ugh!

"Did you hear me?" Turtle Girl's words come out like a grunt.

Nasser places the book on his head and starts to do a shimmy dance. That's when I lose it. Laughter spills out, loud and thunderous, blending in with the noise from the other students in the library.

"I'm so sorry," I say, waving my hand to shoo Nasser away. A thought strikes me: no way this guy is in any way related to the Macoutes. He's way too pure. And dorky.

She turns around, but Nasser returns to looking like the model student that he is. Back all straight, ankles crossed, licking his thumb and turning the page of his etymology book. The boy is probably memorizing the definition of some little plant on Mars.

"Is that your man or something?" Turtle Girl faces me just as Nasser starts dancing again.

The answer gets stuck in my throat. I finally look more closely at her and notice a star-shaped pattern of freckles beneath her left eye.

"He's just some kid." I ain't letting this chick up in my business.

"Wouldn't think Haitian boys would be your type." The accusation comes out in a whisper.

"What's it to you?" Turtle Girl's got my attention now, but she's already rising and collecting her things.

"Where are you going? You didn't even teach me any-thing!"

"I don't think this is going to work." She pulls the

furry hood of her coat over her head, turning herself from a turtle to an explorer in the doggone North Pole. Then homegirl marches straight out of the library.

Mrs. Ruiz calls after her, but she keeps it moving.

"What was that all about, Beatriz?" Mrs. Ruiz comes running up to me like it's my fault that weirdo left.

"Beats me," I say.

And here comes Señor Sabe'todo offering up his two cents.

"That was quite a strange pairing, Mrs. Ruiz. Perhaps I can be of assistance and be a peer tutor for Beatriz?" Nasser sweet-talks the scowl straight off Mrs. Ruiz's face.

It's getting louder by the second in the library. Mrs. Ruiz reminds everyone to keep it down. She looks through her clipboard, her cheeks turning burgundy with the passing of each noisy second.

"If I'm going to try to improve, I can't work like this. Can we study somewhere else?" I ask.

"Fair enough, Nasser. I'll mark you down as a tutor for Beatriz. Be sure to stop by my office this week and fill out the volunteer paperwork."

Nasser gives Mrs. Ruiz a nod as she walks over to a table of rowdy seniors.

"Yo, what was with that girl? You know her?" I ask Nasser as we leave the library.

"Nope, but does it even matter? You should've been matched with me in the first place. Now let's get out of here. I know the perfect quiet spot to study."

REVELATIONS

"BALLET IS THE FOUNDATION of every style of dance there is."
Señorita Amaro paces the large, open space with a long
pointer in her hand.

It's the same stick she has no problem using to pull
our legs forward as we stretch on the barre.

Rumba music plays from the boom box, a welcome,
soothing way to end a busy week. We review each position, starting with our heels kissing in first, all the way to
heel-to-toe feet in fifth.

Then we run through other moves that my legs and
feet and arms have almost forgotten from years ago when
I used to take classes: pirouettes across the entire floor,
turn-turn-turn—*Keep your eyes fixed, Beatriz!*—arabesque
with the front leg bent and the back leg lifted toward the
heavens. *Point your foot, Beatriz—tendu!*

It is like this for an agonizing thirty minutes of class.
A series of reminders of yesterday. A wake-up call of
all I have purposely forgotten, given up. Of all I've missed

that the other dancers, including Nasser, know as easy as breathing.

Every move involves pain, and every pain feels like I'm one step closer to death. Each muscle pulls and stretches to the point that I feel like I'm turning myself into a human rubber band.

Señorita Amaro doesn't pity me one bit.

"¿Quieres renunciar?" She gets all up in my face as my feet relevé to the tips of my toes, arms reaching for the stars.

"I'm no quitter!" I let out a panting breath.

The violins grow louder, faster. And though classical music ain't really my thing, each note brings back memories of when I heard music in everything, everywhere, everyone.

"Take two!" Señorita Amaro calls out, and we scurry to our bags to grab water.

I take a long sip, and the coldness breathes life into every part of me that feels overstretched.

"I told you she was intense." Nasser grabs a towel and wipes the dampness off his face.

"Intense, torture, death. All the same thing," I say, half laughing, half serious.

"You'll get used to it." A girl interrupts us. "I'm Shakira." She holds out her hand for me to shake it.

"Oh, how rude of me! Beatriz, this is Shakira. Shakira, this is my friend from school, Beatriz," Nasser says.

My stomach gurgles when Nasser calls me his friend. I'm not so sure if I like that title. Also, I'm not so sure how I feel about Nasser's *friend* Shakira, with the perfect ballerina bun. But I smile back because that's the right thing to do. I think.

"Nice to meet you," I say.

"You too. You're keeping up nicely."

For a second I wonder if she's telling the truth or putting on a front for Nasser.

"Enough small talk, everyone." Señorita Amaro claps us all back into reality. "Next up is choreography."

For the first part of class everyone was quiet, serious. But when Señorita Amaro mentions choreography, they lose their minds.

"Raise your hand if you're auditioning for *Fame* next Friday," Señorita Amaro says.

Every single hand shoots to the sky. All but mine. Everyone looks at me like, *Girl, are you crazy?*

Nasser presses his hand in the arch of my back, sending electric sparks up and down my spine. My hand joins everyone else's. Pointed up, loud and proud.

"That's what I'm talking about!" Señorita Amaro smiles so deep, I notice the dimple she has in the center of her chin.

"Showing up is only half the battle. Showing up *on time* is the first step." She doesn't look at me when she says the "on time" part, but I already know who it was meant for. I wasn't as late as the first class, but I was still a few minutes behind everyone else tonight.

She paces the room, pointer in hand, continuing her speech. "The casting directors won't care about who can do the highest kicks or who has the perfect pirouette. It's about more than that. It's about the journey. Are you willing to take it?"

Her every word melts into the deepest parts of me. I want it. So bad. I close my eyes and picture myself dancing behind Debbie Allen. Our feet and hands and arms become one with the beat.

"Do you have the fire?" Señorita Amaro screams.

Yes! Yes, I do!

"Up! On your feet! Pay attention, because I'm only going to show you once. No one will coddle you at the auditions."

Señorita Amaro shows us a series of four eight-count moves. Each move different from the next. A perfect blend of ballet, jazz, African dance, and street dancing.

"Miguelito, hit the play button!"

Music fills the space, making its way to my ears, fast-paced, heart-pumping. Together, we begin. *Five, six, seven, eight!* Leap up, bone straight, kick and *pow!* Legs lifting, feet tapping, arms thrusting as we leap through the air.

My eyes are wide open, but I don't see the bodies and the movement around me. Just my own reflection in the mirror. The story that each shape my arms and hands and feet make.

Pirouette! Chassé! Each move takes control. I shift, I stretch, I rock; I dance away the bad. Papi's hitting, Mami's pretending, Junito's hiding, my wrongdoing. Dance away every night that me, Junito, and Mami spent together in Newark, cold, hungry, damn-near penniless, despite the three jobs Mami held down. That island pride would not allow her to accept help from no one. Not from the family that took us in when we first got here. Mami packed us up after a week, moved us to the Grafton Projects. She wouldn't let the government help. By the umpteenth time the lights shut off, Junito knew he had to do something.

Junito got taken under the wing of a guy called Chacho. Folks around the 'hood knew him as a hustler, supplier, and real one-man show. Junito learning the streets from Chacho took us out of the projects, moved us up the hill, helped Mami get the bodega, and got us all a better life. Fly clothes. Street cred. All of it. Within a year, Chacho took off, said it was time to retire. Junito claimed his spot, and the Diablos grew fast as weeds in spring.

I'm grunting now at the memory and the music, which has changed from African drumbeats to Run-D.M.C.'s "Rock Box."

"That's it! I can feel the fire!" Señorita Amaro screams wildly. "Form two lines like they do on *Soul Train*. I'll give each of you a chance to freestyle for an eight count."

We separate ourselves into two equal lines and, one by one, dance the way our heart guides us. Shakira does a series of split leaps from the start of the line to the end. Nasser backflips twice—I didn't know he could move like *that*—and then does a B-boy windmill, finishing with a headspin for four seconds longer than the allowed eight count. The whole class is cheering, though I'm probably the loudest one. I'm so impressed by Nasser that I don't realize it's my turn.

Señorita Amaro points at me. "¡Ve, baila!"

Just then the music shifts to a beat so familiar, so natural, that I don't have to tell my body what to do. Celia Cruz's thick, deep voice begins singing "Quimbara."

It's the same song I auditioned with for the school pageant last year. For eight counts, the world is mine. I close my eyes, curl the tips of my fingers, and arch my back. My feet quicken with the beat as I picture myself floating.

When the last student is done on the Soul Train line, Señorita Amaro lowers the music.

"Excellent job today! Since everyone is auditioning

next week, class will be canceled. Be sure to practice. Also, don't forget to take your headshots with you. That's very important for any audition. Make sure it is labeled with your name and contact information."

As soon as she says that, I realize I don't have a headshot. I got a few pictures of me and my Diablas that we had done downtown at the graffiti wall, but nothing professional looking.

Great. Just another wake-up call that maybe I should give this up.

"I'm hyped up for next week!" Nasser says, packing his things.

"Yeah, me too, I guess. I just need to figure out the picture part."

Señorita Amaro must have overheard me, because she butts in. "I can take a picture of you, Beatriz."

I take a look at myself. Every part of me is drenched in sweat. And I don't need a mirror to know that my hair has turned into a carpet piled on top of my head.

"But I look a mess," I say.

"This is a dance audition. They're not looking for a special type of photo. They're looking for a special type of dancer. You want a picture too, Nasser?"

"Sure, I'll take one." Nasser shrugs.

Señorita Amaro runs into her office to grab her Polaroid camera. Meanwhile I dig through my bag, praying I can find a brush and maybe some lip gloss to help.

The light of the camera flashes in my face as she takes my picture. It takes some time for the photo to develop, the image slowly coming to life. The face that stares back at me is unfamiliar. Happy. Hopeful.

I've only been home a half hour or so when the phone rings ten minutes into studying for Mr. Hankerson's test next week. Shocker that I'm studying on a Friday, I know. Especially after an exhausting dance class. Nasser's been basically kidnapping me every day after school and taking me to the Newark Public Library, and it's apparently rubbing off on me.

"How's the inventory and basement repairs coming along?" It's Julicza.

"Um, yeah, the repairs are gonna take longer than I thought," I tell her.

Translation: setting up my excuse for why I'm gonna miss next week's meeting too.

"Mmm-hmm, I bet." Something tells me that Julicza is smiling on her end of the line.

"What's up with you lately? Spit it out," I say.

"I could easily ask the same thing of you, princesa. Something you wanna tell me?"

Silence. Seconds pass with only background music playing on her end. Héctor Lavoe and Willie Colón's "Todo tiene su final." The same song Junito and I danced to on my birthday.

"Turn it off," I demand.

"Excuse me?" Julicza fires back.

I speak louder this time, just in case she didn't hear me the first go-round. "The song. I said turn it off!"

Is it possible that words can cry? Because that's what my voice feels like in that moment. Maybe Julicza can sense it, because she does exactly as I ask.

"Okay, okay." Julicza softens her tone a notch.

"Did everybody sell their share?" I ask.

"Almost. Juan messed up again. Strike two."

"How did DQ handle that?" I ask.

"Oh, you know exactly how." Julicza laughs. "And since you weren't there, DQ let me take your spot. Next time you see Juan, just know the chichón above his eye was all me."

I swallow hard at the thought. Julicza doing my job. And what do I say to her for bashing Juan in the forehead? *Great work? Well done?* My stomach hurts.

"I'm tired. I gotta go." I yawn out the last few words.

"Tired, huh? From what?"

"Inventory." I yawn again, this time with more force.

"Yeah, I bet."

Julicza cuts the line before I get a chance to respond.

KEEPING SECRETS

UN SECRETO ENTRE DE DOS, se quede entre los dos. Pero un secreto entre de tres, sabe todo el mundo. I think I might be turning into Abuela. Because it's her words that get me through the week. But I've also heard this refrán in English: the secret of two stays between two; but add a third, and a hundred will be all up in your Kool-Aid.

So for now, what I got going on ain't nobody's business: my dance classes and meeting Nasser in the basement of the library, where he tutors me in algebra and adds in some etymology. And thank goodness too, because I'm finally getting the hang of simplifying algebraic expressions.

My tutoring sessions with Nasser are stolen moments where words and poetry and numbers fold into each other, far away from the nosy eyes and ears of any Diablo. And tomorrow? Well, November ninth is the day I'll add to my growing secrets. A day of doing something that's just for me.

Things are looking up lately, and it's hard to hide it.

Dr. Brown catches me in the hall, smiling through my daydream. "Doing better I hear, Ms. Mendez!"

The dismissal bell jolts me back to reality. "Yeah, Dr. B, got a seventy-three on my last algebra quiz. How 'bout that?"

"Not bad. Keep pushing!" Dr. Brown slaps high five with me as I make my way to my locker, happy-dance smiling, not even hiding it.

Julicza, Maricela, and four more Diablas are waiting for me when I get there. As soon as I see them, I remember that I gotta tell DQ that I'll miss the meeting again this week. Up front.

Part of me cares, 'cause I hate keeping things from my girls. But the other part of me doesn't give a flying piece of caca. I'm not missing that *Fame* audition for nobody.

I start coughing uncontrollably. Maricela runs up to me real fast and pats me on the back.

"Yo, Julicza, get that bottle of water in my bag!" she shouts.

But Julicza doesn't move one bit. Tiffany reaches into Maricela's bag on the floor and hands me the bottle. I take a long gulp and let it cool my throat.

"Thanks, girl."

"Not feeling too good?" Julicza asks.

"Yeah, I don't know what's been going on lately, but I think I'm coming down with something. In fact, I'm probably gonna miss school tomorrow."

"Oh, and the meeting, huh? You're gonna need all the rest you can get," Julicza says.

I'm not sure if she's being nice or sarcastic. As soon

as I open my locker, a few of my books and a folded-up piece of paper fall to the floor. My heart stops for a split second, thinking back to the Polaroid picture I found in my locker. But so much time has passed, and I haven't gotten anything else since. I pick up the paper and open it slightly. The first thing I see is the title and author: "The First Day" by Nasser.

"What's that?" Julicza reaches for it, but my hand moves quickly, and I stuff it in my pocket.

"Just some algebra notes from last week," I lie, placing the books back in my locker.

"Oooh, no thanks! It's probably covered in dragon breath," she says, and everyone laughs.

The halls are emptying. At the far end, I catch sight of Nasser glancing back at me. No one else notices.

He's smiling, and the look in his eyes reminds me that some secrets are worth keeping to yourself.

My fingers become a magnet, clinging to the paper in my pocket for the whole bus ride home. My face plays a game of pretend as I smile my way through Julicza and Maricela retelling the best and worst parts of their school day.

My feet fly up the steps to my apartment, hands trembling as I slam the bathroom door, back sliding to the floor.

I drown myself in every word.

The First Day, by Nasser Kervin Moreau, November 8, 1984

On the first day,
you introduced me to the word possibility.
Do you remember that moment too?
How the whole world stopped
beneath our feet
when the music swelled in the room?
Still you push away what's obvious to let in.
Me,
us,

this.
Electricity sparking again, again, again.

REMEMBER MY NAME

I NEVER EXPECTED aNY of this. Auditioning to be an extra on my favorite show in the whole wide world. The dream and my hope fill me up as I stand in line, hands folded into Nasser's. I feel his heartbeat pulse through my fingertips. The audition line is wrapped for what seems like miles.

For two hours we wait among the masses of people. Together we inhale the cold, exhale the nerves. When Nasser and I finally make it inside the school, the first thing the staff tells us is to warm up. We undress immediately, stripping down to our dance gear. Him in jogging pants and a tank that reveals every line and muscle racing through his arms and back. And me in my leggings and leotard, hair clipped into a tight bun on top of my head.

Nasser and I run through a series of stretches, lunges, and positions, just like Señorita Amaro has us do in class.

I scan the room, looking at all the dancers, many a lot older than Nasser and me. I see a few kids from dance class. Having already auditioned, they're walking out, unchosen, hope fading, but still wishing us good luck in a way that feels like they mean it.

"Pin this number to your shirt." A man with a clipboard hands me a paper with the number 307 on it and a couple of safety pins.

"Is Debbie Allen inside?" I ask curiously. The whole train ride here I couldn't help but hope, wonder, and pray that I could be in the same room as her. Let alone dance for her.

But the dude starts laughing at me, revealing a shiny gold tooth right in the center of his mouth. "Not a chance, young lady. The cast rarely attends cattle calls."

Disappointment settles inside me. But I pull it together. Focus!

"Name and headshot, please." The woman standing beside Mr. Gold Tooth holds her hand out for my Polaroid picture.

"Beatriz Mendez." My voice shakes as soon as the words come out, and I already hate myself for not knowing how this all works, even if it is my first time.

The man writes my name down on the clipboard, and he and the woman move on to Nasser.

We're in the next group waiting to dance the routine. Through the glass doors, I can see dancers onstage reviewing the choreography before they audition. I'm not gonna lie, those moves look hard as hell. I look down and beg my feet to remember everything the choreographer says.

"Now when you get in, stay in the back of the auditorium while the dancers audition. The choreographer will cue when it's your turn to go onstage. You guys ready?" Clipboard Dude yells.

"Yeah!" all of us scream at the top of our lungs. He pulls open the double doors as if they are a portal to some magical kingdom. And in a way, they are. The stage is massive, hovering over hundreds of seats. The walls are lined with posters of some of the cast. Jesse, Ian, Coco, Leroy, and of course *the* Ms. Lydia Grant—*my* Debbie Allen!

The dancers are onstage dancing as if their lives depend on it.

I stand there dreaming, squeezing the life out of Nasser's hand.

"I know, I know. This is *crazy*!" he says, his eyes almost as wide as mine.

"I'm five seconds from passing out." I take a deep breath and take in the moment. The music cuts off just as the dancers hit their final position.

The choreographer yells out, "We'd like numbers 291 and 299 to stay for round two. The rest of you, thank you for your time and have a good evening."

Just like that, people's dreams are flushed down imaginary toilets, and I start to feel like maybe I need to leave before I even start. What made me think that a couple weeks of dance classes would be enough to pick back up where my training left off?

"Next group!" The choreographer yells for us to come onstage.

"That's us." Nasser gives me one of his flashy, happy-go-lucky smiles.

The choreographer separates thirty dancers into three rows of ten. Nasser and I are placed in the last line. Fine for Nasser. He's tall. But I'm so short I can't see much. We run through the steps. Eight counts of pirouettes, four grapevines, two back-to-back jump splits, with a split land on the floor. This is all to be done three times, with each line switching at the end of the set.

The choreographer's every word, every move, comes out like lightning.

"Music, please!" he yells, and the signature *Fame* song starts to play.

This is it! This is my shot. My eyes find their way to the ceiling, and I whisper a prayer to the heavens. ¡Ay Dios mío! Please don't let me mess up!

Irene Cara's voice fills up the room as she sings about wanting the whole world to remember her name. The countdown begins, and my arms and feet and heart remember every move. It's as easy as breathing. The lines shift through two sets of the choreography, and finally my turn in front arrives. There is a table with five judges seated at it, eyes locked on us, their hands scribbling on clipboards, taking note of our every move, never looking down, not even for a second.

I could stay like this forever, dancing to the music, smiling like I've never smiled before, tasting the air of dreams and possibility trapped in that room. But just like that, the final move takes it all away. The music cuts, and the judges at the table clap and hand the choreographer a sheet of paper.

"We would like the following dancers to stay: numbers 306, 320, and 312."

Three dancers step forward. Poised. Experienced. Older. Not me.

I refuse to breathe. If I do, I'm sure I'll shatter into tiny pieces right there on the stage.

We are rushed out of the auditorium after that. No second chances. Just a thank-you and a good-bye. Hope floats itself right out of me. But I don't want it to leave. I want to run back in there and feel the music again and again until they really *do* remember my name!

"Hey, now." Nasser grabs both of my elbows and pulls me in to his chest. Even his sweat smells good. "Chin up. You were amazing."

"And so were you," I say in a half whisper.

"That's show business, you know. You win some, you lose some. But at least you're back in the game."

We pull our warm clothes over our dance clothes, put our jackets on, and prepare to brave the cold streets of New York City to head back to Penn Station.

"You did a good job back there." A dancer stops us before we leave. "I'm Alejandra. What's your name?"

As soon as we introduce ourselves, I recognize Alejandra.

"You were picked from the group before ours, weren't you?" My eyes light up.

"Well, for the next round, but who knows what'll happen after that. They might make us do a style of dance I'm not so good at, like tap. The last three times I auditioned for *Fame*, I didn't get called. Maybe fourth time's the charm?" She winks at me.

The reality sets in that I got a long road ahead if I'm gonna keep following this dance dream. I just don't know how long I can keep all this under wraps.

"I hope you guys don't give up," Alejandra says.

"She won't," Nasser says.

"She? What about you?" Alejandra asks.

"I'm more of a 'jack-of-all-trades, master-of-none' kind of guy. I dabble in a few different forms of art. But Beatriz has dance flowing through her veins."

"Yes, I saw that. Where do you study?"

"Well, I took a few classes in South Orange when I was younger, but then I stopped." I hesitate. "Because things got busy . . . with school." *And being in a gang.*

"But she's back at it now. She's studying with me at the Newark Community School of the Arts." Nasser throws that in.

"You guys are from Newark? That's dope. Me too!" We all slap high five.

"When I was in high school, there was this contest I did, and it had all these different categories. One of them was dance. I even won the gold medal for it. You ever heard of ACT-SO?"

Ding! Ding! Ding! There's those familiar letters again!

Nasser loses his cool and throws his arms up. "Yes! That's what we can do next. Remember I told you about this a while back, Beatriz? I can enter the poetry category, and Señorita Amaro can choreograph something amazing for you. You might have to switch your days though, for private lessons."

Alejandra points at us and says, "Definitely do it. It's a good line on college applications. Plus, if you win the local contest, you get to go to nationals. And that's like nothing I'd ever experienced. I'm telling you, folks like Magic Johnson from the Lakers were there, and I met Sheila E. This was a few years ago, before she made it big. Doing ACT-SO will get you ready for more auditions like this too. Think about it."

"Yeah, I definitely will." I sigh out a mix of worry, pride, fear, and hope all over again.

When they didn't call my name for the next round of *Fame* auditions, I started to tell myself that this is it, back to my normal life as a Diabla. But it's looking like this dance dream won't die out just yet.

SUSPICIONS

CAREFULLY, I CLOSE THE front hallway door behind me before heading upstairs to our apartment.

"Where you been?" The darkness covers us both, but I can make out DQ's voice from anywhere.

"Yo, don't sneak up on me like that." The pace of my heartbeat dances a fast eight count.

The floor beneath his feet creaks as he walks closer. Outside, the street lamp flickers, flashing a piece of light right on the side of his face.

"You miss a couple meetings 'cause you got stuff going on here that needs taking care of. I can live with that. Earlier, tú me dijiste que estabas enferma." DQ raises his fingers and does air quotes. "But you looking pretty healthy to me, creeping in late, coming from ... where *are* you coming from, princesa?"

Most of the time, the big-brother act is cute. Amusing. Welcome. But not today.

"Took a walk. Needed to clear my head." I fix my best

no-estoy-mintiendo expression on my face and fumble with the keys to open the mailbox.

But I can tell he doesn't believe me.

"Must've been a *loooong* walk." DQ takes one hand and sticks it in his coat pocket.

I stop breathing for a second, maybe ten. "I don't know what you're talking about." My lips quiver out the words. "I'll be at the next meeting. Promise."

DQ strokes his goatee with one hand, his other still tucked in his pocket.

"I hope you mean it, 'cause we got some big scores coming in. Y ¡mira! If you don't want in, I can think of *someone* who will."

DQ reaches out and grabs me by the elbow. Not rough, but not gentle either.

"Is there something going on that you ain't telling me?"

"Nothing's going on. It's all good." The lie comes out easy as I yank my arm away.

"Cool." He nods. "Tell your abuela that she should be more careful about leaving the door unlocked."

DQ slams the door and leaves me standing in the hallway. Alone.

After taking a shower and rifling through my bag and a pile of school stuff, I find what I'm looking for. I sit on the floor next to Junito's altar, staring long and hard at the ACT-SO form. Am I really gonna do this?

And on the inside, a tiny voice whispers back, *Of course you are.*

❁ ❁ ❁

REGISTER FOR ACT-SO TODAY!

WHO WE ARE: Created in 1978 by journalist Vernon Jarrett, ACT-SO is a program of the National Association for the Advancement of Colored People (NAACP). ACT-SO stands for Afro-Academic, Cultural, Technological, and Scientific Olympics. It is a student enrichment program that culminates in local and national competitions where high-school students compete for awards and prizes totaling more than $100,000.

ELIGIBILITY: Our contest is open to high-school students of African descent in grades 9 through 12. Students who participate may compete in up to three categories, which include the sciences, humanities, and performing and visual arts.

The top three medalists from the local competitions in each category will advance to the national contest in Dallas, Texas, July 12–14, 1985.

The local competition will take place March 23, 1985, at Arts High School, 550 Dr. Martin Luther King Jr. Blvd., Newark, New Jersey, at 9:00 a.m.

Fill out the registration form to reserve your spot in the local competition. Deadline to apply is December 1, 1984.

Name: BEATRIZ MENDEZ

Address: 712 BROADWAY, NEWARK, NJ

High School: BARRINGER

Grade: 9

Grade Point Average: D+ (WORKING ON IT)

Category of Competition: DANCE

Mail form to: Newark NAACP, 454 Washington St., Newark, NJ 07104

"BELIEVE IT, ACHIEVE IT, AND ACT-SO!"

THE ART OF HIDING

HiDiNG iS aN aRT FORM in itself. To be good at it, you almost have to find the perfect balance between making yourself visible and invisible at the same time. For the next few weeks, that's exactly what I do.

Slip into school and make myself seen by Mr. Hankerson, Mrs. Ruiz, and especially Dr. Brown. Study in the late-night hours when the world is sleeping. (I'm actually starting to like it too!) Distribute the product like a chameleon. Hide from Nasser at school, which, given how big Barringer is, ain't a problem. Finish that ACT-SO application, slap a stamp on the envelope, stick it in the mail. Go to meetings, now at DQ's spot, since the basement is "under construction." Show up to dance classes . . . late. Retreat to the storage room when Mami and Abuela are asleep and practice everything I learn from Señorita Amaro. Leave everything I'm hiding right there on the floor. Let my feet, my arms, and my hands do the talking and the dreaming.

But all good things come to an end. Even hiding. The phone rings at five after nine, just after *Fame* ends, after I get Mami to bed.

"I'm sorry, Beatriz. Is it too late to call you?" It's Nasser.

"Well, you know a girl does need her beauty sleep," I say.

"What'd you think of tonight's episode?" he asks.

"Dr. Scorpio was on an ego trip. Did you see those alien costumes?"

We both start laughing at that.

"Say, Thanksgiving is coming up."

Talk about changing the subject. I don't need the reminder. It'll be our first Thanksgiving without Junito. There were other holidays before this one, obviously, but this will hit hard. Thanksgiving was always a big deal in our house.

"Yeah, I'm looking forward to it," I lie.

"You should come to my house for dinner," he says. "You can bring your family."

So they can freak out when they find out that I've made nice-nice with someone from the same culture as the person who killed Junito?

"I don't know about that." Even the thought of all of this might be too much for me.

"Just think about it. I want you to meet my family."

I pause for a while, not responding.

"Beatriz?"

"Yeah?"

"When are you going to let me in?"

"Into what? What are you talking about?"

"I want to get to know you. . . . Like, the real you. We've

been dancing together for a while now, and when we do it's like you're releasing all this pent-up emotion, except I don't know what those feelings are. You tell me we can't talk at school. I don't know your friends, and they don't know me beyond calling me nerd boy when they see me in the halls. But when we're alone, it's a different story." He finishes his long speech and the line goes quiet.

Everything he is saying is true. I haven't told my girls anything about Nasser past that one time they saw him trying to step to me at my locker. And with the way DQ is acting these days, telling him is out of the question.

"I can hear you breathing, Beatriz. I want to get to know you better. What are you hiding from me?"

"Nothing," I say. *Everything. I'm hiding everything.*

"If you change your mind, I'm at 823B South Sixteenth Street. Six o'clock, Haitian time."

I laugh at that one. "I'm pretty sure Puerto Rican time is the same thing. So if I come, I'll see you at seven thirty."

Nasser laughs too. "Whatever you decide, I hope you have a good Thanksgiving, Beatriz *Ayita* Mendez."

The hope in his voice remains in my ear long after he hangs up.

AN UNLIKELY THANKSGIVING

ABUELA AND I GIVE Ms. Geraldine and her daughters Thanksgiving off. They'll join us later for dinner, since the rest of their family is back in the Philippines. Abuela and I open up the bodega only until five. Even DQ is in the holiday spirit. He tells the Diablos they can take a couple of days off to spend time with family. No standing outside hugging brick walls. No drug deals. No Friday meeting. Just quality time with the ones they love.

We barely get any customers in the bodega, but like always, we stay open for those who forgot eggs, bread, or milk.

I woke up at the crack of dawn to get the turkey going in the oven in the bodega and put the pernil in the oven in our apartment. That pork shoulder and turkey will be falling off the bone by the time dinner rolls around. All that's left to make is rice and beans and tostones.

Mami stays inside the apartment all day now, milk crate planted by Junito's altar, staring out the window.

Five o'clock comes fast, and we start closing up shop. Abuela sweeps the floors, empties the cash register, and lowers the blinds on the windows. I grab the keys to lock the door. As soon as I turn off the lights and start to walk away, I hear a swishing sound.

"¿Qué es eso?" Abuela stops in her tracks.

Even though the store is dark inside, the flickering streetlights show exactly what was just slid under the door.

A Polaroid picture.

"It's nothing, Abuela," I lie. "Vete arriba."

She leaves for the apartment upstairs, and I race to unlock the door and dash outside. No one is running. All I see are cars driving by and an older couple holding hands at the bus stop.

I go back inside, lift the picture off the floor, and damn near drop it when I see the image staring back at me. It's Mami, sitting outside—milk crate pressed against the brick wall, face pointed to the sky. She has no clue that someone is taking a picture of her. And what's even more strange is that there's another message written in Creole: "Kisa ou genyen deja."

The last picture of me and Nasser had "Kisa ou vle" written on it, meaning "what you want." I've memorized that phrase by now. *Kisa* and *ou* are the same. So this is "what you something." And it's all too much.

Not to mention the words the dude whispered to me all those months ago: new pop blay. I need to ask Nasser what those words mean. But how, without telling him where I heard them? Now this photo has Mami in it. What does this all mean?

I had stopped worrying about all this, but something about this picture rattles me to my core. I close up the store again, head upstairs, slip the picture in my coat pocket, and don't say a word to Mami or Abuela.

Ms. Geraldine, Liezel, and Ninita, arrive for dinner right on time. They bring a pot of pancit, a Filipino noodle dish, to add to our holiday meal.

When six o'clock rolls around, the bell rings. I'm not expecting anyone else, but I shiver at the thought that whoever slipped that Polaroid under the door might be back. Maybe this time for something more face-to-face.

"Who is it?" I ask through the buzzer.

"It's Daniel Martin. . . . I just want to drop something off for your mother and wish her a happy Thanksgiving before I travel tomorrow."

Abuela mouths, "¿Es el poeta?"

"Yup, it's that wanna-be Langston Hughes." My words come out annoyed.

"¿Quién?" Abuela's confused as all get-out. But then her eyes brighten and she squeals, "¡Invítalo!"

"Come on up, Mr. Martin." I press the buzzer to let him in.

She rushes to open the door and stands in the hallway, waiting for Mr. Martin like a little kid waiting for Santa Claus. I stare at her, thinking of her backcountry mindset, of "mejora la raza." How that's had me confused all these years.

In true Abuela fashion, she whips her neck at me, probably reading my mind.

"¿Qué? I didn't say anything."

"No estoy ciega, Beatriz. But you know what is blind?

El amor y la amistad. Even an old lady like me can see that now."

Mr. Martin heavy-foots his way to the top of the steps, and Abuela greets him with a big hug and a thousand "mi amigo lindo" kisses.

Mami's face lights up as soon as Abuela leads Mr. Martin inside the apartment.

Abuela speaks in her best English: "Mirta, she waiting for you every day!"

"Sorry I haven't been coming as much. I've been doing a lot of overtime hours at work." The whole time, Mr. Martin's bending over and hugging and greeting Mami, Ms. Geraldine, and her daughters, and it's like I'm not even here.

"Would you like to eat with us?" I ask.

Abuela doesn't even give the man a chance to say no. It's a funny sight, seeing her little self yank Mr. Martin into a seat at the table. Next thing I know, we're taking turns saying prayers in English, Spanish, and Tagalog, and passing around our plates.

Nobody says much, and I'm not sure if it's because this is completely awkward or if it's that the food is just that dope. So I decide to break the silence.

"Where's your family for the holiday?"

Mr. Martin's black eyes pierce right through me. I already know where TJ is. San Francisco, where Junito should be.

"Pop is out like a light. Ate his dinner early."

"And your daughter?" I still can't bring myself to say her name, especially after what went down between us last year.

"Vanessa's at a chorus competition in Florida. I'm flying

out tomorrow after work to see her compete." He looks at me straight on.

"Wow, she's really doing her thing, huh?" I'm not really that shocked.

"Yeah, straight A's, still singing, doing great."

All of that cuts me . . . deep. She did exactly what she said she was gonna do. Follow her dream. Do something with her life. I made those same promises to myself. But at some point, I just . . . gave up.

When we're done with the food, Abuela starts washing the dishes and putting them away. Ms. Geraldine and her daughters head back home.

Mr. Martin and Mami are seated on the couch. He hands her a journal, covered in pressed flowers.

"What's in that book?" I ask as Mami turns to the first page.

"A poem written by my daughter, with some blank pages for Mirta to fill in, if she wants. Just a little something to get her through. Vanessa wanted her to have it." Mr. Martin looks up at me.

I lean over and take a peek, but Mami speed-reads and turns the page before I can finish. That fires me up something good, but I refuse to show it. I'll just look at it later when Mami goes to bed and Mr. Martin is long gone. Of course Vanessa would do something nice like write my mother a poem, even after what I did. Once upon a time, Mami loved Vanessa like a second daughter—made dinner for her, gave her pads when she got her first period, helped her with her Spanish homework. Even after all this time, after the loss of her own son and the silence, I'm certain Mami still cares for Vanessa.

Together, Mr. Martin and Mami look through the blank pages, each one bordered in a different type of flower. With her fingertips, Mami traces the shapes of pointy sunflowers, purple bell flowers, and rounded wishmaker flowers with their petals floating down to the end of the page. She does this for a while, silent and hypnotized, until she falls asleep with a smile planted on her face, journal pressed to her chest.

Mr. Martin stands up and starts to put on his jacket. "Well, I better be headed off to work."

Abuela yawns and thanks him for stopping by.

It's still early for me. I don't want to go to bed. Plus, I got something I need to take care of and it can't wait. "Mr. Martin, think you can give me a lift?"

He looks at Abuela, waiting for her to object. "Where to? I'm not sure if your mother and grandmother would want you going out this time of—"

"Abuela, ¿puedo ir a la casa de mi amigo Nasser?"

Of course she gives me the full interrogation: ¿Quién es ese amigo? What kind of name is Nasser? Why haven't you told me about him before? And who leaves their family on Thanksgiving night?

I tell her everything she wants to hear: that he's the smartest student at Barringer; that I'm going to be with his family, not just him; that he takes dance class with me; and that he tutors me in math and helps me learn big fancy English words like *pulchritude*.

That's enough to satisfy her.

"She said it's fine, Mr. Martin."

"That was a lot of Spanish for just 'it's fine.'" This dude annoys me to no end.

"If you can't take me, I can just catch the bus."

"Buses never run on time on holidays. I left my car parked down the hill on Grafton. Let me grab it, and I'll meet you back here in ten." He walks toward the door to leave.

"Thanks, I'll be right down."

Mami's closet is full of beautiful skirts and dresses of all colors, heels and platform wedges sitting on her shoe rack, collecting dust. Her dresser is stacked with lip gloss, blushes, and bottles of flowery perfumes that haven't touched her skin—or mine—in months. The second I start transforming myself, I'm asking myself why. I smooth some gel on my edges, run a brush through my forest of hair, and tie it up into a ballerina bun. For the first time in a long time, I like the image that's staring back at me in the mirror.

Mami clutches her flowered journal to her chest as I tuck her into bed. I kiss Abuela good night before she heads into her bedroom.

"Tan bella, princesa." She rubs her fingertips across my face and I feel the beauty in her touch.

"Nasser's phone number and address are in my drawer. If anything happens . . ." I suddenly realize I shouldn't be going out. That's it. I'm staying.

"Nada va a pasar, Beatriz. Now go, enjoy."

"Be home by 10:30," I promise.

I shut off the lights after she walks away, slide the blade in my cheek, triple lock all the doors, and slip away into the dark.

BETTER LEFT UNKISSED

WEIRDEST. RIDE. EVER.

Mr. Martin and I don't speak beyond me giving him the address. Luckily the roads are mostly empty, and we get there in no time.

I thank him for the ride, and the car hovers in the middle of the street because he's refusing to move until he's seen me go inside.

The first thing I hear when I ring the doorbell at Nasser's house is music. Soul-stirring, hip-swaying, earth-spinning beats that sound so similar to the sounds of my island, but I don't understand the lyrics.

The door swings open and it's a girl, probably about eight or nine years old. As soon as she sees me, she says, "Are you Ayita?"

"Umm, yes, Beatriz Ayita," I clarify.

Then she screams over the music, "Nasser's girlfriend is here!"

I stare at her.

Nasser hops down a whole flight of steps, loses his balance, and pushes the poor girl out of the way.

"Hey, you're here." He stands tall and adjusts his tie, like he didn't just almost bust his ass.

"Ooooh, she has on lip gloss and a dress!" the little girl says.

"Don't mind my little sister, France. Come in." He deepens his voice and leads me to the second-floor apartment.

The smell of pure heaven hits me hard the second he opens the door. Pork, rice, plantains—the aromas of the Caribbean. His house is packed with people dancing, singing, and eating.

"You have a big family, Nasser." I get close to his ear so he can hear me over the music.

"Honestly, I don't know half of these folks. My mom invited every Haitian she's met from here to Elizabeth since we moved to Newark."

I hold my breath for a count. *Shit. Could there be Macoutes here then? The girl with the ice-blonde dreads?* But I don't have time to worry because Nasser starts introducing me to everyone. There have to be at least forty people in the house. Two Uncle Jeans, three cousins named Esther. By the time we get to the fifth Aunt Marie, I've already lost track of who's who. That doesn't stop me from greeting them with a hug and a smile.

Nasser's mom lights up when she sees me. Pulls me in close for a hug and sways back and forth to the rhythm. Then she grabs my face with both of her hands and speaks in Creole.

I look at Nasser for a translation.

"She says she's heard so much about you, that it's nice to finally meet you, and she hopes you enjoy the food and kompa music."

I feel the pink in my cheeks surface. Nasser's family sure knows how to make a girl feel special. Little France offers to help me make a plate.

I place some fried chunks of pork on my plate.

"This is called griot." France is having a good time playing teacher. She adds a large spoonful of black rice—diri jon jon—and fried plantains that we call tostones, but Haitians call banan peze. When we get to the end of the line, I see a bowl of something that looks like a salad.

"You like pikliz?" France asks.

"Pickles?" I ask, thinking that is what she's saying. But it doesn't look like pickles. It looks more like cabbage.

I grab a few shreds from my plate and take a bite.

"Wait, that's not what you think it is, Ayita!" France squeals.

Flames shoot up my nose the instant the pikliz hits the back of my throat. I scream with my mouth open so wide, the blade falls out and lands in my hand. I look at France to be sure she didn't see it. She's already headed for the kitchen. No one else notices either. Someone shuts off the music and turns on the lights.

"Quick, get her something to drink," Nasser yells, while a crowd gathers around to stare like I'm possessed. I don't need a mirror to know that my skin has turned devil red and I've grown a sweat mustache. I'm coughing while carefully slipping the blade into my dress pocket. Mrs. Moreau grabs a Bible and starts fanning me with it. France pushes back through the crowd and hands me a cold glass of milk.

The whole room grows silent, waiting to see if I'll pass out and be labeled the first case of "death by pikliz."

"Woo-hoo! That was good and *spicyyy!*" I yell, in spite of my scorched throat.

Everyone starts laughing and clapping.

"Oh yeah, she's an honorary Haitian now!" Aunt Marie number four calls out.

The music kicks in again, and everyone is back to eating, laughing, and dancing in the darkness. I can't remember the last time I had lots of family over like this to celebrate. Actually I do remember. April. Fairmount Cemetery. Tearstained faces on cousins, aunts, uncles, Abuela, Mami. No Papi, of course. Don't even want to think about all that. Not here, while the kompa music pours into me.

Nasser reaches his hands out for mine. Our foreheads press together. I can feel the heat on his skin. His eyes are closed. He extends our arms out together, and leads us against the rhythm. Round and round he spins me, never loses count. He dips me low, and my ballerina bun comes undone and my hair whips against my shoulders.

I transport myself to the audition for *Fame.* Those lyrics from the song that breathe life into this very moment: *I'll learn how to fly.* And those moves that sent me spinning, kicking, soaring. That feeling of wanting the beginning to begin again. On the dance floor, I can empty out everything that is bottled up inside of me—anger, pain, joy. Tonight, right there in the middle of Nasser's living room, dancing among his smiling aunts, uncles, and cousins, I choose joy.

Next thing I know, Nasser's family makes a circle

around us and cheers us on. I hear Nasser's dad telling them that we auditioned for "that famous television show," and how next we're going to do a big competition called ACT-SO. Everyone oohs and aahs and smiles in approval.

I lose count of how many styles of music we dance to. All I know is, my feet are pulsing in these heels, I've sweated out Mami's best dress, and it's already past ten thirty. Nasser leads me to the bathroom before I get ready to go. I wipe the sweat off my face, rinse the blade in the sink, and slide it back in my mouth.

Nasser's mom won't take no for an answer when I try to turn down the tray of food that she wants me to bring home to my family.

"Pran li, no!" Mrs. Moreau says.

Nasser nudges me in the ribs. A subtle warning that this will be a battle I'll lose if I don't give in quickly. I thank Mrs. Moreau for the food and hospitality. The room is swollen with even more people now. I make my rounds, hugging almost every single person, until I get to the last one, hidden in the darkness. She's not looking at me. Her eyes are fixed on Nasser. As soon as I try to lean in and get a better look, a dancing couple bumps into me. And the girl slips down the hallway, toward the bathroom.

"Who was that chick running away like that?" I ask Nasser as we walk to his dad's taxi.

"I'm surprised you didn't recognize her . . . your original *tutor*," Nasser says with a laugh.

"No way! Oh my goodness, what was her name again?"

"Ha! You think I remember? I was kinda' busy charming you that day."

Damn. There's that smile again.

"Please don't tell me that you're related to her!" Now I'm laughing and reliving the memory of her morphing from a human turtle to a North Pole explorer during our failed tutoring session.

"That'd be a hard no. I don't know when she showed up. I told you my mom found every random Haitian in a twenty-five-mile radius and invited them over. Now all of a sudden I've got a host of fake aunts and cousins. A lot of my actual family is still back in Léogâne."

"Well, she sure was staring at you like she wanted a piece. I think someone has a secret admirer!" I start tickling Nasser's neck.

His laughter starts up again, sending his breath swirling up to the cold, late-night sky.

Nasser walks to the passenger side, opens the door, and laces his icy, gloveless fingers into mine. "There's only one person I admire."

I'm not sure what to do with that, so I just stand there telling myself, *Don't look at his eyes, don't you dare take a peek!* But my hardheaded self doesn't listen.

He's absolute night-sky-coated, moon-speckled perfection.

"After you." Nasser holds out his hand for me to take a seat.

By the time he reaches the driver-side door, I can finally breathe again. He starts the ignition and turns on the radio. Stevie Wonder's "I Just Called to Say I Love You" comes on.

Nasser starts singing with the music. High and super loud, it sounds like a wolf's mating call. Laughter rolls out of me, hard and nonstop.

"What? You don't like my voice?"

"I thought you said you could sing. You should stick to dancing."

With his eyes fixed on the road, Nasser leans sideways toward me so I can hear the words loud and clear. "My folks really like you, Beatriz."

"Well, I like them too."

"And what about me?" he asks.

My stomach starts to dance that flip-flop move. He slows the car at a red light and locks his fingers in mine, wrapping me in his warmth.

"I'm falling for you, Beatriz *Ayita* Mendez. And I'm just wondering when you will admit it."

"Admit what?" I ask, not letting those fingers go.

"That you like me too."

I'm laughing all over again. But I'm not making fun of him. It's more like *I hate that you're right so I'm gonna fake-laugh my way through this ridiculously uncomfortable moment.*

Nasser makes a right onto Springfield Ave, and the car behind us makes the same turn.

"I do like you, Nasser. I just need to take my time right now. I have a lot on my plate."

"No pressure here. I'll wait as long as it takes, so long as I know you feel the same. I want to get to know you. I want to meet your family and get to know your friends at school. No more hiding."

The car is still behind us, inching closer and closer. And then all of a sudden the driver shuts off the headlights.

"Nasser, I need you to take a detour." I turn to face the back window.

"Oh, you're playing this take-the-long-way-home game again?"

The car moves in closer.

An icy chill runs through me. "Make a sharp left. Step on it!"

He does, confused as all get-out, until he also notices the car tailgating us.

"Do you know this person? My dad will kill me if I get so much as a scratch on this taxi."

I wish I could say that it was DQ acting all loco because I'm in a car with a guy who's not a Diablo. But I know that's not the case. DQ is in Brooklyn, having dinner at his abuelo's house. I try to make out who's behind us. Look for the slightest trace of something familiar. A yellow bandana? A halo of dreadlocks outlined in the shadows? Nope. Nada. Just a soft glow of moonlight around the driver's faceless head.

I'm not even sure what to tell Nasser. The truth? He doesn't know about Junito or the gang or any part of my drug-dealing life. I can't. I can't let him know that stuff about me. Not after I just told him I like him and that maybe we have a chance to be more than friends. I wouldn't know what to call it. A relationship?

"Just turn here, up Jones Street. It's probably like a drag-race challenge."

Nasser slams off the radio button and starts speaking real fast.

"You know, I saw on this show *20/20* that gangs do this sort of thing. They turn off their headlights and chase people down the street, trying to cause them to get in an accident. It's like some gang initiation or something."

I feel sick the second he says the word *gang*.

We're real far from Broadway now, heading down Route 21, yellow reflectors on the road zipping past us. I tell him to get off at the next exit. That doesn't throw the car off one bit. Ahead I see the flashing lights of cop cars. Only then does the driver swerve left and leave us alone on the road.

Nasser slows the car and parks a few feet away. He feels safer here, I guess. Me? I don't do police. The quicker I can get home, the safer I will be.

Nasser shakes his head and grabs my hand. "I'm so sorry you had to go through that just now."

Bro, I've been through worse. "It's cool. We're fine."

"No, it's not cool. Don't get me wrong—I'm happy my family moved here, because I would've never met you—but the gangs, the drugs, the violence, is just as bad here as it was in Miami." He says that last part with disgust in his voice, and suddenly I feel like the lowest, foulest creature that's ever existed.

"And you'll never believe what I heard at school."

"What's that?"

"Barringer High has its own drug ring going."

I almost spit my blade out of my mouth—again, twice in one night. But instead I cough real loud.

"Can you believe that?" Nasser slaps me on the back. "That's what I get for keeping to myself. What idiots would have the nerve to sell drugs right on school property?"

I wish I had an answer for him. Something to explain why I'm in that life. And why I can't easily get out.

Instead I mumble, "Well, you can't believe every rumor you hear."

"Ha! Rumor? I saw it with my own eyes in the boys' locker room. Some kid named Tony Pedros was doing a trade-off. I couldn't believe it!"

I try to stop the cringe before it reaches my face. Note to self. Give Tony a friendly reminder to be more careful.

"Speaking of lockers . . ." I change up the convo real quick. "I got another Polaroid. Only this time I didn't find it in my locker. Someone slipped it under my door at home."

I pull the picture from the pocket of my jacket. "I'm sure it's not the yearbook committee who took this photo."

Nasser turns on the light and takes a look.

"It's a picture of my mom." *Looking crazy as hell*, I want to add.

"I see where you get your beauty from. Do you understand the caption?"

"Not really, that's why I wanted to show you. I know the *kisa* and the *ou* are 'what' and 'you.'"

"Kisa ou genyen deja. 'What you have,' as in, what you *already* have."

"I don't understand any of this. First a picture of me and you that says 'what you want.' Now one of my mom that says 'what you have.'"

"Actually, this is kind of sweet, if you think about it. Maybe one of your friends took the picture when you weren't around?"

"But my friends wouldn't do that without telling me. They know better." Not to mention I don't have any friends who know Creole. Other than Nasser, that is.

I take in a deep breath and beg myself not to cry.

"My mom hasn't been herself since . . ." It's a release

to start to admit it, even though my tongue stops me from saying the rest. And then suddenly I can't stop the tears.

"No, no, no. Don't cry." Nasser wraps his arms around me, pulls my head to his shoulder, and I swear it's like that shoulder was made just for me. A perfect fit, my face nestles in the softness and hardness of it all.

We sit there in silence, him letting me cry and whimper without asking me one question. How is it possible that he hasn't heard about my brother's murder? Granted, it's been a while since the papers have written about it, probably because a trial date hasn't been set yet. Plus, I guess keeping my distance at school is working—nobody notices we're friends, so nobody's fed him that little tidbit.

He turns the radio back on. Cyndi Lauper's "Time After Time" is on. Our arms wrap around each other, not ready to let go, even after the song fades to a commercial. I want him to hold me like he's doing and tell me that it gets better than this.

I lift my face up to his and on the inside I'm saying, *Don't kiss him, don't kiss him*, but my lips find my way toward his. Like two magnets, the force can't be stopped. I could say this was my first kiss, but that would be a lie. In seventh grade, I kissed this boy Curtis on a dare. The only snaggletoothed twelve-year-old I ever met. Neither of us knew what we were doing. And boy did I ever regret it when he slipped his lizard tongue into my mouth!

But this? This is different. Natural. Meant to be. Our lips touch, and I part my mouth like they do in the movies. He slides his tongue into my mouth. But the second he does, I close in and he yelps. When he pulls away from me, I notice a tiny dot of blood on his bottom lip.

"I'm so sorry, Nasser." I slide my blade farther back with my tongue and frantically search the glove compartment for a tissue.

"I'm good, Beatriz." He places the tissue on his lip, and the speck of blood disappears. "First kiss?"

"Maybe."

Maybe not. Ugh!

"It's all good, but boy do you have some sharp incisors." He's laughing, but I want to disappear.

We don't see the plainclothes police officer walk up to the car, but we sure hear him bang on my passenger-side window, startling us out of the moment.

I roll down the window, seeing only a bearded mouth beneath a large hat.

"You guys live around here?"

Nasser leans toward the window. "No sir. We actually thought we were being followed a few blocks back, and when we pulled in this area, the car went the other way. We're just about to leave, sir." He's got that white-boy voice down pat.

Number one rule of the hood, Nasser. Never, ever talk to five-o. This boy from Haiti by way of Miami has a lot to learn.

"Following you, huh? We suspect there's some gang activity in the area, so I suggest you guys—" And then the officer bends down to face us both.

He tips his hat up, and I recognize those bushy eyebrows right away. Detective Osario. Judging from the way he's studying my face, I can tell he's trying to remember my name.

"Don't I know you?"

"It's Beatriz." Nobody asked Nasser to chime in.

"Ah, yes! Mendez. Well, surprise, surprise. It's been a while." A sly smile dances across his face.

I clear my throat and think about how to play this out. "Detective." I nod.

"Oh, you know my girlfriend?"

My eyes widen. *Wait, your what?* And I swear I see that same question on Detective Osario's face.

"Are you related or something?" Nasser says with a cheesy smile.

Detective Osario chuckles, but I don't find anything funny. "No, son. Ms. Mendez, you wouldn't happen to know anything about what's going on around here, would you?"

Nasser looks concerned, and I guess he feels like he has to keep speaking on my behalf.

"Gang activity? No, sir. Beatriz isn't into that. And me either."

Detective Osario gives me a major eye roll that I pray Nasser doesn't see. He taps the car door. "Yes, of course. You two should head on home. Stay safe now."

Nasser extends his hand across me to shake the detective's hand. "Thank you, sir. You have a happy Thanksgiving."

The detective throws me a wink that says, *I guess your little boyfriend is clueless, huh?*

Nasser turns the car in the opposite direction and heads back down Broadway. The whole time I'm having a Beatriz vs. Beatriz moment in my head.

Thought #1: What would Nasser do if he discovered the real me?

Thought #2: It might be time for you and homeboy to take a break. He's getting way too close.

Track Four: Dance of the Bolero, Winter 1977
In the battle to stay awake to cast out the memories, sleep wins. Always.

It never snows in Puerto Rico. But here in Newark, land of streets and cars and urban rhythms, the snow is falling outside our window. A tiny window in a tiny room in a tiny apartment on top of a liquor store in the Ironbound of Newark.

The same little apartment that was filled with at least twenty or thirty people when we arrived from the airport. Strangers who greeted us with worried smiles, served us a spread of Portuguese food, spoke to us in a language so similar to Spanish, yet so different. And when the sun left the sky and the snow began to fall, they wished us all the luck in this new place to call home as they left.

If only I could be outside with the snow falling on my face. I'd give anything for the coldness to melt into my tears, take away the heat building up fast and bold.

Mami and Junito are sleeping, folded into one another on a mattress on the floor, pressed against the window wall. Mami cried for hours until she ran out of tears. Junito pressed his face against her chest, not shedding one tear, looking at me as if he were made of stone, until he too closed his eyes for the night.

It is past two in the morning, long after the time I should be asleep. But the tears and fears and nerves take over. I'm worried about what lies ahead. New school. New people. A test. Failure?

What will the kids think of this Puerto Rican girl who looks like the people roaming the streets of Newark but can't fix her lips to hold a conversation, let alone make friends?

The bedroom door creaks open, startling me out of my thoughts. A young woman's face peeks through the door, whispering in Portuguese.

"Olá, sou Fernanda. Acabei de chegar e queria conheê-la."

My brain tries to process what she means—I can sort of understand her. I didn't see her earlier. Why, I'm not sure. Maybe she wasn't here. It doesn't matter anyway because the flight, the arrival, all of it is a foggy cloud hovering over me.

She walks slowly toward me as though she's dancing the bolero, each step long and slow. Under the moonlight her ice-blue eyes and almost-too-blonde hair glow brighter as she comes closer.

"Não chore." She kneels in front of me, wiping my tears with the back side of her hand.

"Pero . . . me . . . quiero . . . ir . . . pa' casa." I follow each word with a whispered sob.

She pulls a strand of hair behind my ear and draws me into her chest. "I remember when I first came here from Portugal. I was scared, just like you."

"Yo . . . quiero . . . mi . . . papi . . ." Confusion and anger boil up inside my eight-year-old body. Old enough to understand why we left. But not enough to change how I'm starting to feel about Junito. We could have stayed. Junito could have tried harder to not make Papi upset. It could have been different.

"If it is meant to be, you will see your papi again." She

places my head on the pillow, pulls the blanket over my shoulders.

Ronaldo pokes his head through the door. "Fernanda, let her sleep. She has school in the morning."

"Coming, uncle!"

She gets up, taking the moonlight with her, but stops short at the door and whispers, "I promise you it gets better."

I wake up, tossing and turning in bed. I never laid eyes on her again. La blanquita with the piercing eyes and gentle words. But as I lie in bed, thinking through the memory, I realize that she was wrong about two things.

I never saw Papi again.

It didn't get better.

ACT THREE: BECOMING

THE DAY WILL COME,
WHEN YOU REMEMBER
NOT WHO YOU ONCE WERE,
BUT WHO YOU ARE BECOMING . . .

—VANESSA MARTIN, SEPTEMBER 1, 1984

DEAR MRS. MENDEZ,
I ASKED MY FATHER TO GIVE THIS JOURNAL TO YOU
ON A DAY WHEN YOU NEEDED A REMINDER THAT THERE'S ALWAYS
A REASON TO BE THANKFUL. I CALL THE JOURNAL DARLENE, BUT YOU
CAN NAME IT AS YOU PLEASE. MAY YOU FILL IT WITH SINGING,
DANCING, AND SPEAK-WORTHY WORDS.

—NESSY

ONE WORD AT A TIME

SALES ARE UP AT Barringer, just in time for the Christmas holiday. I have my runners to thank for that. It's lunchtime and a crew of us are chilling at our spot behind the school. Past the parking lot, past the cluster of bushes, where a few feet away, a concrete wall stands between the grass and the highway. Far enough away from Mrs. Ruiz and nosy-behind Dr. Brown.

It's cold as hell, but we don't care. Tiffany is tagging up the wall with the Diablo signature. A red pitchfork with streaks of gold weaving from top to bottom, outlined in black. Maricela is flirting with Mooki, but what else is new? Julicza is blasting Whodini's "Five Minutes of Funk" from a boom box. And in the midst of that bass pumping through me, I'm kicking it with Tony, showing him a sample of DQ's new product, Sour Diesel.

"This stuff is gonna make us serious bank!" I tell him.

"Word." Tony smiles, his teeth looking too big for his mouth. Then he pulls me in for a hug.

"Oh, that right there would make a dope pic! Hold up!" Julicza screams over the beat. She runs to her backpack propped against the cement wall.

I back away from Tony, cold air running through me. Next thing I know, Julicza's got a camera in her hand. A Polaroid camera.

Like a magnet, my legs pull me toward Julicza, eyes fixed on the camera I never knew she owned. Skin tingling, insides twitching, my mouth is like a gun popping off in rapid fire.

"Where'd you get that?"

"What do you mean?" She takes a step back.

"The camera," I snap.

Pause. Confusion. "Um, the store."

Eyes roll. Not mine.

"When?"

Laughter. Also not mine.

"I *just* bought this." More laughter. Julicza throws Maricela a look I can't read.

Eyes back on the camera. Worn, scratched up. This chick is lying.

My hand becomes a claw, Julicza's shirt and flesh caught in its grip. The crew is on me now, pulling me away, screaming, "Yo! Chill, princesa!"

"Why would you take a picture of my mother?"

Tears building. Lips quivering. Mine. Hers too.

"What are you talking about?" she asks.

Music off. Voices, whisper-soft. *Beatriz is losing it for real.* Arms wrap around my waist, hands pressed in the arch of my back. It's Tony. Again.

"Cálmate," Tony says.

Inhala. Exhala. Just like Mami always used to tell me.

There's a bend in the bushes. And out comes Nasser looking like a fake-ass Inspector Gadget. Our eyes lock. I die a little on the inside. How did he find this spot? He stands there, staring, heat building, until he finds the will to speak.

"Can I talk to you for a second, Beatriz?"

Tony loosens his grip. "Who's this pendejo? You need me to handle him?"

Nasser's leg is shaking now, palms pressed together.

I take one step forward, but Julicza blocks my path. "I didn't take any pictures of your mother. Why would I do that? I mean, not with the way she . . ." Julicza can't find a nice way to finish the words.

"Yeah," I choke out. "I found a recent picture of her, and I don't know who took it."

"Well, it wasn't me." The red in Julicza's eyes deepens.

Maricela steps in between us. "Julicza stole that rag-gedy thing from the quarter bin at the thrift store last week. I was with her. Are you okay, Beatriz?"

I blink and shift my eyes to Nasser. Julicza takes my hands in hers, squeezing them gently. Something about it takes me right back to when we were eight years old, skipping rope in the Grafton parking lot.

I look at my crew, pucker my lips up, and as if on cue, they all head back in the direction of the school.

I push my hair forward to hide the red in my eyes, the stain on my cheeks. I turn to Nasser, finally. "What's up?"

And sure enough Nasser hits me with the full-on in-terrogation. "Why haven't you been answering my calls? Why were you yelling at them just now? Why are you crying? And most importantly, why was Tony Pedros holding you like that?"

Questions mixed with sadness, concern, jealousy. But it's just all too much for me.

"Can we do this later?" I ask. "And did you follow me out here or what?"

"I'm starting to hear things, Beatriz."

"Like what?" I blink, trying to clear my head of what just happened.

"That some of your so-called friends are in a gang. That got me thinking. Ever since I met you, you've made all these rules. Don't talk to you at school. Don't hang with you at school. Basically, make myself invisible unless it's for your benefit, like tutoring at the library or dance class. And you know what? I'm starting to piece it all together. You. Them. Just hanging out while your friends spray the word *Diablos* and that symbol on the wall?"

"Look, they're harmless. Just chill."

"I still don't understand why you haven't told them about us. What are you, ashamed? Because I'm not like other guys at this school? Is it because I'm Haitian?"

That last part hits me in the gut. "No, that's not it. It's just . . . well, I don't like people in my business. Plus, I kind of like the way things are." I slip my hands around his waist, but he moves away cold and quick.

"You mean you like to use me when it's convenient for you. Yeah, I get it."

I can smell his disappointment. "Nasser. I promise I'll call you later . . . okay?"

"Au revoir, Beatriz." He slips through the trees and back toward the parking lot.

I never understood the power of good-bye until Junito died. And as I stand there, watching Nasser and that voice of his and his words float away, I am reminded of how long a good-bye can last.

I gotta get out of here. Now. I head straight to my locker to grab my things and do what I used to do best: cut.

Stuff goes crashing to the floor as soon as I open my locker. I'm picking things up and what do I find? Polaroid number three. I turn it over and see the face of a guy that I've never seen before in my life. Light brown skin. Hazel eyes. Good-looking. Definitely not as foyne as Nasser. The message below says, "Kisa mwen pap jamn jwenn anko."

This is twice as long as the last two messages. What you want . . . what you have . . . and now this new confusion? Starts with *kisa*, though.

Selfishly, I'm wishing I hadn't fought with Nasser. I need him to translate this for me. I tuck the picture into my bag, wondering how to fix this. And us.

Julicza rolls up behind me just as the next bell rings. "We cool, right?"

"Yeah. Just forget about earlier." I shrug it off. I need more time to process everything.

"What did nerd boy want?"

"Don't call him that," I snap.

"Well, excuse me, nena. You don't have to hide it anymore."

"Hide what?"

"That you like him. I can see it in your eyes."

"Well, I'm pretty sure I'm not the only one hiding things." I slam the locker shut.

I leave Julicza and her mouth standing right there. Speed out of the back door by the gym and make my way to the bus stop, heat racing through me. I haven't decided if I believe Julicza's story yet. I get these mysterious Polaroids and all of a sudden she's got a beat-up looking Polaroid camera? Plus she's all up DQ's ass and stepping to my role in the Diablas at the same time? Maricela and I been cool since day one, and I never knew her to lie to me. Still, something's not sitting right. I need someone to talk to. Someone to help carry the weight of all this. These secrets.

DQ is standing outside the bodega when I hop off the bus. As soon as I see him, it's like the voices in my head split in two. *Don't tell that pendejo nada*, part of me cries out. But the other half, the one who feels my insides breaking apart, says, *He might be all you got.*

"We need to talk ASAP. Meet me downstairs in ten," I say with some fire in my voice. I don't stop to see if he's surprised that I'm bossing him around.

I go inside the bodega and check on Abuela and Ms. Geraldine. They say they're fine. Tell me it was busy earlier because everybody is starting to buy their Christmas food. But the rush settled down a few minutes before I walked in.

I sneak downstairs, praying with every step that nosy Abuela isn't following. I don't have time to deal with her Spanish proverbs right now. DQ is already waiting at the back door for me by the time I get there.

I open it and he slips in.

"Guess these basement renovations are coming along nicely," he says, looking at the unmoved pipes and tools on the floor from his last visit.

"Whatever." I pull back a chair, slamming the legs down before I gesture for him to take a seat.

"And you might wanna think twice how you talk to me, especially in front of the crew. Anyway, what's this about?" DQ falls slowly into the chair.

"I didn't want to come to you with this, but I don't have a choice." I pull out all three pictures and place them on the table in the order I received them.

DQ shifts his eyes to the photo of me and Nasser, then back to me.

"I'm not sure what these pictures mean, and I need you to help me figure it out," I say.

DQ picks up the first Polaroid and brings it in close to get a better look.

"Who's this dude up on you?"

Oh, now he wants to play big brother again? Not interested. "It's this kid from school. We were taking some stupid ballroom dancing lesson in gym class."

DQ cocks his head to the side.

"Whatever, yo. Just move on to the second picture," I say.

DQ tightens his lips around his teeth.

"Oh yeah? You been off your game lately, and now I see why." DQ flicks the picture, and it lands on the floor.

We stare at each other long enough to expand the space between us. Breath caught in my lungs, I think of the last time I exhaled free and clear. Not with him around. It was those stolen moments on the dance floor. Just me and Nasser and rhythm and not one care in the world.

I lean down to pick up the picture. "I said move on."

I grab the second Polaroid and shove it in DQ's face.

"Someone took a picture of Mami"—and then I hold up the third picture—"and who the hell is this guy, DQ? And don't you lie to me!"

DQ pulls the two pictures from my hands and places them back on the table, leans back in his chair, and rubs both hands over his shiny bald head.

"Where did you get these?" he asks.

I tell him about the first time I received a picture in my locker. And about the times I thought I was being followed. How someone slipped the second Polaroid under the bodega door on Thanksgiving. And then this final one. Received conveniently after I find out that Julicza's got a Polaroid camera.

"Julicza ain't part of the equation, so cancel that." DQ spreads his arms out, thick veins running from his wrists up to his neck. "But you've been keeping this in all this time?"

"I was just trying to protect—"

"Protect who, Beatriz? Yourself? Cause you definitely weren't thinking about the Diablos!"

"You weren't there that day, DQ! And you don't know what it's been like watching my mother, trying to keep her and my family safe." Hot tears of rage are building up.

"Describe the person who followed you on Thanksgiving." DQ doesn't care one bit about my tears.

"I don't know. It was dark, and the headlights weren't on. I couldn't see. What does all of this mean, DQ? Tell me. ¡Ahora!"

"This language . . ." DQ's voice trails off.

"It's Haitian Creole." I translate the first two pictures for him. And I admit that I have no clue what the last picture says.

"When did you pick up another language, princesa?"

"A friend helped." My pulse pounds through the half-truth. I can almost see it through my skin.

DQ cups his face in the palms of his hands. "I'm gonna tell you who the dude is in this third picture, and what I think about all of this, but don't freak out, okay?"

I steady my breath and get ready for him to hit me with the craziness.

"As you know, the night before Junito was killed, we went to the South Ward to pay a visit to the Macoutes chief, Gaston."

"The guy Junito offed," I say. My heart detonates as I remember finding out that Junito had actually killed someone. And that's what got him killed.

"Yeah. They were trying to take over our territory, and Junito wasn't having it. We got him when his boys weren't paying attention. The dude in this photo is Gaston Mondesir."

"Wait! You never told me his last name. He's related to the dude mentioned in the paper? Clemenceau Mondesir. The one who killed Junito." I'm shaking my head, hoping this is all some sick joke.

"¡Cálmate, Beatriz!"

"Don't you tell me to calm down!" My hair is wild now, covering half my face. "This Clemenceau dude has been stalking me from behind bars because of something Junito and you did!"

"Doubt it. At first I was gonna say that maybe he was behind this. I mean, Gaston was his brother. But these pictures and messages feel personal, almost too planned out. Most dudes wouldn't go through all this trouble, rivals or not. We'd just come out full force, none of this calculated, creative stuff."

I recall the fire-red kiss blown at me before the car left behind a cloud of gray dust. The flash of yellow in the dismissal crowd. The times I thought I was being followed. And the one real time, when I know that car was following Nasser and me.

"It's her."

DQ twists his face. "It's who?"

That's when I spill out the rest of what I've kept bottled up all these months. When I finish, I look at DQ.

"So maybe it's the girl with the dreads? Could she be the one behind all this?"

"Maybe, but when's the last time you seen her?"

"The day Junito died . . . at least that's what I thought." I can barely get the words out because a feeling takes over. Three parts doubt. One part *but what if*?

Doubt wins. It can't be her. It's been months, not to mention that even if it was her at school on the first day, she was running away from me.

"I don't understand why you didn't come to me with all of this sooner, Beatriz."

"Oh really, DQ? No estoy ciega." I'm channeling Abuela now, fingers snapping all up in his face. "You don't think I see what's going on with you and Julicza? How you're basically pushing her into my spot?"

Right there, I'm expecting DQ's face to soften.

"Oh come on, princesa, I got eyes on these streets! You think I don't know what you been doing, or should I say *who* you've been doing? Don't try to act like you ain't out there losing your focus. So of course I gotta weigh my options."

"What are you trying to say, DQ?"

He points to Nasser in the picture. "Word has it you been extra busy these days. Taking dance classes . . . with this Haitian boy, apparently. Funny that while your little friend was translating these threats, maybe he's the one behind all of this. That's what you get for hanging around the enemy!"

I'm in race mode now. "You don't know what you're talking about, DQ! Nasser's not like that! He doesn't know nothing about drugs or gangs."

How did we go from blaming the blonde-dread chick to pointing fingers at Nasser? How could I have been so stupid? I should have known that DQ's been watching me. Keeping score. Taking notes. Thinking Nasser is a problem. Well, DQ is dead wrong.

"I don't want you seeing this guy no more. I say you figure out if your little tutu ballerina classes are worth it."

"You can't tell me what to do!" I'm screaming now. "You're not my father or my brother!"

Now DQ's up and screaming. "Well, I'm the closest thing you got. Junito is gone! Your papi ain't around. Your mami won't say a word to you or nobody." He inches his face so close to mine, I can smell last night's rum on his breath.

"And you should probably open your eyes some more because your little friend would be more than happy to weasel her way into your top spot. All you got is me!"

"¿Qué está pasando ahí abajo, Beatriz?" Abuela's voice echoes through the locked door, down the stairs, forcing us both into silence.

I point to the back exit without saying anything else to DQ. He gets up, raises his hands in surrender, and nods his head at me as he walks out to the alley.

I lock the door behind him and run heavy-footed up to the bodega, reality setting in that I can't trust nobody. Not DQ, not Julicza, nobody. Why did I even think I should tell him any of this?

Just before I run all the way up to the apartment, I see a woman standing outside with her mouth pressed against the bodega window. Her hair is a mess, stretched every which way. She's dressed in a torn trench coat so dirty, I can't even tell what the original color was. Under that, she's wearing jeans and a bra. In December. There's a little boy, no more than three years old, next to her who's holding a G.I. Joe toy.

"Beatriz!" Abuela shouts out my name while slamming a chancleta against the window. That does nothing, because the woman outside just starts licking at the sandal through the window.

"¿Quién es esa mujer?" Abuela asks.

I tell Abuela not to worry and head outside.

"Get outta here!" I yell at her.

She stops licking the window and stares at me with wild eyes. She looks familiar, like underneath all the crazy I once knew her, but I can't put my finger on it.

She scratches at her neck before speaking.

"Heard y'all got some of that new stuff," she whispers, like it's the best-kept secret in Newark.

"Whoa, I don't know what you're talking 'bout."

Never, ever, ever have we had a customer roll up on us at the bodega. That is law and everybody knows it.

All the while the little kid is staring at me with the saddest eyes I've ever seen. Underneath the sagging flesh on bone, blackened lips, and glossy, red-veined eyes,

I realize I do know the woman. She had the honor of jumping me in to the Diablas. Nixida Vigo. Well, what's left of her.

"This your little boy?" I ask.

"Yeah. Say hi, Beto."

Little dude throws me a shy wave and a look that begs me to pull him from the storm that is his life. A pain shoots straight through me. Not long after Nixida jumped me in, she broke a major Diablo rule. She started using and got hooked on the very thing she was supposed to be selling. My last memory of Nixida was the sound of her screams and the sight of four Diablas pouncing her. I ain't seen her 'round here since.

"Sooo . . . no more playing around. How much? I ain't got a lot to pay. Just need enough to take the edge off," she says.

Pain turns to rage. Rage shifts to my hand, and I yank her by her filthy collar so she can be close enough to feel the heat of my words.

"Lay off that stuff, Nixida. Look at what you got." The tears sting as they fall down my face. "Now go home, put some clothes on, and take care of your son."

Beto starts whimpering, and I immediately loosen my grip.

"Don't cry, little man. I was just hugging your mami because I haven't seen her in so long, that's all. Right, Nixida?" The fakest smile plasters itself on my face.

She lets out a hacking cough. "Yeah, that's right. Come on, we gotta go."

She buttons her coat, grabs Beto by the hand, and makes her way down Grafton Hill.

When I get upstairs, I see Mami sitting on the couch, writing in the journal Mr. Martin gave her. When she sees me fly through the door, face stained up, she puts her pencil down. I storm off to the bathroom to wash the filth that is Nixida off my hands. Then I stomp to the bedroom and throw myself on the bed, burying my face in the pillow to mask the screams and the ugly truth of what I have become.

Mami comes into the room holding the journal in her hand. She sits on the bed next to me, at first letting me have my release while she rubs my back. Up and down, until I feel I have no tears left.

Then she gets up, turns on the boom box, and pops in a tape. One Way's "Lady You Are" comes on, slow and hypnotizing.

The music fills the room, and Mami lifts my chin so I can look her in the eye. Then she says her first word in eight months.

"Baila."

My shoulders collapse at the sound. I'd stopped believing that the day would come where I would hear Mami's voice again. But there it is, raspy and hard, like sun-scorched grass begging for rain. I grip my arms around her tight, not wanting to let go. She rises slowly, taking me with her. Leaving her book of words on the bed, she grabs both of my hands. And then she leads me to the windows where the curtains are open and the setting sun is pouring in. We sway to the beat. I rest my head on my mother's shoulder. More tears come; this time, happy tears. And I become a little child all over again, remembering the days of music and laughter on our island far across the Caribbean Sea.

The song ends, and Mami rewinds the tape.

"¡Baila!"

I dance with her once more, letting the light fill in the dark spaces, happy to get my mother back, even if it is one word at a time.

FORGIVENESS

EVERY TIME I call Nasser, he isn't home. Whenever I look for him at school, he's nowhere to be found.

It's not until after school on the last Friday before Christmas that I find him, tucked behind a shelf in the back of the Barringer library, reading a poetry book. Typical.

I say nothing at first. Just look over his shoulder as he reads "Fire and Ice." It's almost like I can see the words float off the page, into him, into me. Each word a reminder that both fire and ice are necessary for survival.

"That's beautiful," I say, breaking him out of his poetic trance.

"Yeah, Robert Frost is one of my favorites," he admits, closing the book.

"Looks like you've been hiding from me all week." I playfully tap him on his shoulder, and he moves away from me like I have some kind of contagious disease.

"Just returning the favor."

"Come on, don't be like that." I lean in for a kiss, but Nasser wants no part.

We sit there, the silence multiplying around us. I examine every inch of him. That ebony skin, those brown eyes sliced with speckles of gold and green. And his smell. Man, I miss the way he smells.

"I'm sorry."

The corners of his mouth twist. "Tony Pedros is your type. I get it. So you don't have to worry about the disintegration of your reputation."

This kid ain't never gonna speak in plain old English.

"Tony is like a brother to me." I laugh a little. "You caught him holding me back from fighting. It's not like we were kissing and hugging."

I reach for Nasser's hand, but he just yanks it away. And he's not smiling either.

"If you came to ask about tutoring, you're good to go. It looks like your average is improving so you won't be needing me anymore."

Nasser starts packing.

"I need your help," I say, hoping that'll slow him down a bit.

"Seems like that's all I'm good for with you." He zips up his backpack.

"I promise you that once I show you this, I'll tell you everything."

The librarian, Mrs. Arcentales, finds us hidden behind the shelves. "Guys, it's so lovely to see you two enjoying a book of poetry, but it's Christmas break, for crying out loud. Don't you want to go home? Because I know I sure do."

"Sorry about that, Mrs. A. We'll be leaving now." I nudge Nasser in the ribs.

Mrs. Arcentales twists her lips. "Beatriz Mendez, right? I think your name is on the list for the peer tutoring program."

"Yeah. Nasser is my tutor. Right, Nasser?"

He flashes a fake nod-and-smile.

Mrs. Arcentales quick-steps to her desk, grabs a sheet of paper, and comes back to give it to me. "You should consider joining the Freeform Poetry elective next semester. I'm teaching poetry in a new way. Almost like music, pouring your emotions on the page. It'll be a good way to bring up your GPA. Think about it?"

I grab the flyer, questioning how I'm supposed to add this new task to my ever-growing to-do list.

"Sure thing, Mrs. Arcentales. Can't wait!"

Nasser walks out of the library ahead of me, storming out the front door. Feet flying, I huff and puff trying to keep up with him.

"Wait up, Nasser!" I cry out.

His eyes remain straight ahead, not even looking at me.

"Let's go to the Chicken Shack. I promise I'll be quick. And then you won't ever have to deal with me again . . . if you don't want to."

The cold winds pick up. Nasser pushes his gloveless hands into his pockets.

"Ten minutes," I beg.

We walk into the almost-empty restaurant and place an order. I grab a booth by the large window, overlooking the busy street. Nasser comes back with a feast: two grape sodas, buttered biscuits, steak-cut fries, and an eight-piece bucket of deep-fried heaven. But I'm too wound up to take one bite.

"So, what kind of help do you need?" Nasser pops a fry in his mouth.

I open my backpack and pull out all four pieces of the puzzle. First the words, as I remember them, that Clemenceau whispered into my ear. On the piece of paper I wrote them on as soon as I got home from the hospital. Been tucked away in my drawer, not that I would ever forget them, though. Then the two Polaroids with the messages he's already translated. And finally the latest picture I received in my locker.

I slide the paper his way. "What does that mean?"

Nasser lifts it up and twists his face. "New pop blay? Where'd you get this?"

"It's not something that was written to me . . ." My next words come out hesitantly. "They were said to me. I wrote them the way they sounded. Maybe it's spelled wrong, and I think I'm missing a word."

Nasser fans the paper back and forth, whispering the words over and over again, adding his Haitian accent to my poorly written English spelling.

"New pop? Blay? Wait. I think this is supposed to be *bliye*." He pulls a pencil from his backpack and goes into teacher mode, crossing out letters, until the sentence comes out fully formed.

"Nou pap bliye? That means 'we won't forget.' But you said there was a missing word. Are you sure it wasn't 'nou pap janm bliye'?"

The words crash into me and spin me around.

"That's it!"

Nasser's face lightens one shade.

"Beatriz, that's almost like a threat. 'We'll never forget.' That's what it means. Who said that to you? And why?"

I clear my throat, grab the paper out of his hand, and place it next to the photos. I'm trying my best to play it cool as I unlock this mystery.

First it was *We'll never forget.*

Then it was *What you want.*

Followed by *What you already have.*

"I need to know what the latest picture means." I slide it over to Nasser.

"It says: 'What I'll never get back.' But you still haven't answered my question."

Ignoring him, I repeat that translation in my head over and over again. Junito killed Gaston. Clemenceau killed Junito. There is a third Mondesir out there with a message—three messages—just for me. A reminder that they haven't forgotten their promise.

"Beatriz, what's going on? Seriously, enough of the secrets."

It's starting to get late. There's less movement on the street. People are headed home to get ready for Christmas.

"Whatever it is, you can tell me." Nasser's got this caring look in his eyes. "I can handle it."

"I should go." I begin to rise from the booth.

"These threats are similar to something my family has been through."

Now he's got my attention.

"How so?" I ask, sitting back down.

"Back in Haiti, my dad had a good job working for President Duvalier. But when Duvalier's military started executing and kidnapping people, my dad quit. Then, Duvalier's son, Baby Doc, took over and things got real bad. If anyone spoke against his regime, their lives were in danger. That didn't stop my dad, though. We started getting notes nailed to our door, almost like these"—he gestures to the Polaroids—"but worse, signed in blood. So when I was four, we fled Haiti in the middle of the night with nothing but the clothes on our back. We left so fast, I didn't even get a chance to put shoes on." Nasser stops to take a breath.

I should probably stay and tell Nasser everything. He deserves that much. But there's this sound going off inside me—a hushed *tick, tick, tick*—a passage of time that's making my skin crawl.

"Good story, but really, I have to get out of here." I mean it this time.

"Whatever it is you're not telling me, nothing can be worse than what we went through with the Tonton Macoute."

That last word floats in the air and stays there echoing until it explodes between my ears.

"What?" My body jerks, almost knocking the fries off the table.

"And you have the nerve to accuse *me* of keeping secrets!" My voice sounds like it's been electrocuted.

"What? What secrets? Like I owed you my family's backstory, when you never told me yours?" Nasser's mad. I've never seen him really mad.

The people behind the counter stop working.

"I have to go." I gather everything up, stuff it all in my bag, and zip up my coat to face the cold.

Nasser is a force. He stops to throw out our trash, and then flies behind me out of the Chicken Shack. "So that's it? I share a piece of my life with you and somehow I'm in the wrong?"

His words, the Christmas lights, the cars whizzing past lose focus around me. The bus stop is a few hundred feet ahead. I just need to get there.

A swift grasp of my hand halts my speed. My body whips around to face Nasser. Eyes locked, knees pressed against each other, we take turns inhaling and exhaling.

"You're in a gang, aren't you? That's what you've been hiding." His words are an uppercut.

I can't look him in the eye anymore. Instead, I scan the road for the bus, counting how many lights before it gets to me. Four to go.

My mouth opens but stiffens into the shape of an O. No sound. No words. All stuck inside.

"I—"

"You know what? I don't even want to know. I'll tell you this though. You're better than that. It's a shame you can't see it." Nasser peels away from me and heads in the opposite direction.

Three lights down.

"Says the boy whose dad was a Macoute!" If this were a movie, a bolt of lightning would pierce the sky.

Nasser turns around. "Were you not listening to my story, Beatriz? Do you realize the pain it took for my parents to leave our country and entire family behind? The things I do to make sure their sacrifice was not in vain? And you have the nerve to think I'd ruin my future by being connected to some punk-ass gang?"

He says "ass" with a z at the end. The boy can't even curse right.

Nasser flails out his arms, waiting for me to say something. And even though I want to believe him, I can't find the right words to say. Disappointment settles on his face and he walks away once more.

"Go on!" I yell at his back. "I'm used to people leaving me anyway. I'm a Diabla! I don't need you!" The words slip out bold, fiery, scared.

Nasser turns around, his jawline clenched hard. "You've been lying all this time. And I guess your lies include how you felt about us, about me."

"What? No. That part was real—is real." My voice softens.

"Was. Past tense. You had it right the first time," he says.

The bus pulls up, double doors fly open, holiday music pours from the radio.

"You getting on or what?" the driver asks.

My whole body goes limp as I climb on and she closes the door between me and Nasser.

The Macoutes wrecked my family too. I want to tell him this. Make him understand.

I press my fingertips to the glass and close my eyes, imagining Nasser running after me as the bus slowly pulls away. Like they do in the movies when lovers break up to make up. But when I open my eyes, all I see is Nasser pushing through the crowd. He doesn't look back for me. Not even for a second.

ALMOST HOME FOR CHRISTMAS

THERE'S BARELY ANY passengers on the bus. Just a couple of guys in the front and an old lady dozing off in the back seat. I take a seat in the middle row just as "Jingle Bells" switches to "Another Lonely Christmas" by Prince. Well, ain't this a trip. As beautiful as that song is—the guitar piercing through my skin, Prince's voice, like sugar, sweetening up the air—it's the last thing I want to hear. I don't need another reminder of what I'm going through. How I'm facing yet another holiday without Junito. And just when I thought I had one thing going right with Nasser, I went and messed that up too.

Broadway is lined with Christmas decorations everywhere. The nighttime sky makes the lights sparkle even brighter. I look out the window and all I see are happy faces, hopes, and Christmas wishes and possibilities. And maybe it's the sight of it all that makes me think of how I can make things right. For me. For my family. I take a deep breath and make a mental list.

Step 1: Get home to Mami and Abuela and figure out a way to fill our house with the holiday spirit. Invite Ms. Geraldine, her daughters, and Mr. Martin too.

Step 2: Think about how to make things right with Nasser. He's not a Macoute. And I wasn't lying about how I feel about him.

Step 3: Quit the Diablos.

In that order. It's a fairytale vision. But I need some-thing—anything—to hold on to right now and help me forget the threats, the Polaroids, the confusion that's lived in me since April thirteenth. Soon as I get home, I'll get the tree out of the closet. Mami, Abuela, and I will put it up and decorate it. Over the weekend, I'll shop for everyone's gifts. Come Monday, I'll make a spread that shows the best that Puerto Rico has to offer. My signature pernil because who doesn't love pork that falls off the bone? Arroz, pasteles, coquito, and tembleque for dessert.

Abuela and I are gonna tear that kitchen apart! Maybe Mami will even help. Our friends won't know what hit them.

As the bus gets closer to home, I see flashes of red and blue several blocks ahead. Not in front of the bodega, more at the corner of Grafton, a little farther down.

"Looks like there's something blocking the next stop, folks," the bus driver announces. "We'll have to take a detour."

She makes a sharp left on Verona, close enough to home but still a bit far away. As I get off the bus with a few other people, she wishes us a Merry Christmas.

The guy in front of me says, "Feliz Navidad."

I respond too and keep it moving.

Verona is a side street with a couple of apartment buildings and abandoned houses. Two guys from the bus walk so fast they disappear out of sight. I look behind me, and I see a lady dressed up with a huge coat and an oversize scarf and hood on her head, slowly trailing behind. As cold as it is, I almost envy her for looking much warmer than I feel in my short bomber coat.

When I cross at the light, I notice there's a road blockade and flashing lights everywhere. My number one objective is to always stay as far away from five-o as I can. So I decide to take the roundabout way and cut through the train tracks.

A spider-walking feeling creeps up my spine, though, and something tells me to look behind me again. When I do, the lady is walking faster, following me toward the tracks. I'm damn near jogging now, moving toward the abandoned buildings behind the bodega. But the closer I get, the far-ther away home seems. Usually there are folks on the tracks, skipping rocks, making out with their novios, and racing trains. But now there ain't nobody around.

Straight from a horror movie.

I look back again and see her eyes blazing beneath the moon. She rips off the part of the scarf that covers her mouth, revealing fire-red lips puckering straight at me underneath the streetlamps. My tongue races around my mouth, franti-cally moving my blade. I slip my fingers in, pull it out, and grip hard. My feet push harder, faster, and my head turns one last time to see she's running too, whipping off her head wrap, ice-blonde dreads breaking free, beating against her shoulders with every pounce she takes.

I cannot find my voice. I want it, but it's buried deep inside me. My head is swirling. The girl in the getaway car. The girl who's been sending me these threats.

Home is not close enough. Not a Diablo in sight. Just me, her, and the moon following us under the cover of the blue-black sky.

"Sispann kouri!" I know she's speaking Creole, but I don't know what the hell she just said, and honestly I don't care. All I know is that if I go harder, faster, stronger, I'll get to my people, and they'll handle the rest.

She's gaining an edge on me. Her breath is so close I can hear it and smell it. A swift punch knocks the wind out of me, sends me crashing to the ground, flinging my blade into the grass.

Flash! Click! I see the blinding light of a Polaroid taking a picture of me lying on the ground.

"Nou pap janm bliye! We'll never forget what your gang did. I know you ordered the hit on my brothers, both of them!" She towers over me like the Statue of Liberty.

I don't have time to think. I use my leg to give her a swift kick to the crotch. That makes her throw the camera to the ground, grab her girl parts, and wince in pain. My feet turn to wings, flying up and landing in a full squat. My hands follow, throwing several punches to her gut. All the while I'm screaming with each blow: "I . . . did . . . not . . . order . . . any . . . hit!"

Reality unfolds fast and furious. Both Gaston and Clemenceau are this chick's brothers. *Were?* DQ ordered the jail hit, even though I told him to wait because I wasn't sure if I wanted more blood on my hands. Is Clemenceau dead too?

She lunges, knocking me flat against the train tracks. My head hits the iron rail, and I see stars flying high in circles.

I scream. No words, just sounds. Earth-shattering. Loud. My fingers trace the grass, searching for my blade in the darkness. But I am too late.

She slaps. I bite. She rolls. I choke. She squeezes. Kicking, punching, biting, back and forth. We're two rabid wolves fighting for our packs. She pulls away as I claw my nails at her face. One of her dreadlocks catches in my hand. She lets out a loud "*Gahhh!*" as the rest of the dreadlocks fall to the ground in a heaping wig pile.

A single light from the freight train draws closer, shining in all of its glory on her face. A familiar image appears. A star pattern of freckles beneath her eye. A dark bob cut brushing against her ears.

It's the math tutor, the girl who was at Nasser's house, the one who literally turned herself into Turtle Girl right before my eyes. Quiet. Invisible. Calculating.

She hovers over me and spits in my face. Translation: *Yeah it's me, pendeja!*

"You're the one who's been stalking me?" My back springs up fast, bringing a world of dizziness inside my head. I whack her jaw, and blood erupts through her clenched teeth. The train chug-a-lugs closer, screams a hoot into the cold air.

She returns the favor, landing an uppercut right under my chin. I hear the cracking inside my head. Two or more teeth make their way out of my mouth and onto the ground.

I'm fighting with everything I have inside me, but she's not giving up for one second. In the midst of the battle, police lights flash in the distance. There are no crowds to break us up. Everyone must be at the top of Grafton

Hill with whatever's happening that made the bus have to detour.

The train is even closer now, filling our bellies with thunder and our eyes with light. She picks up something. I don't know what it is, maybe a branch or broken piece of the train track, and delivers one final thwack upside my head.

I don't see the stars and the birds and the waves immediately, probably because the train's light is so in my face that all I can think of is hurtling myself away. A few inches too close to death, I pull her with me, and we both go tumbling from the fast-moving train. Our bodies roll and roll until they can move no more.

I lie there, tasting the blood in my mouth, excruciating pain quaking through my head. I try to calculate who will deliver the next blow. But all I hear is the rhythm of our breathing. First fast like a perfect salsa beat, then slow like samba.

I hear her crying before I feel the warmth of my own tears falling.

"He was my brother!" She sobs through every word, each one slamming against me like a ton of bricks.

Just then, I remember her name. Amy Marcel.

"And you don't think I miss my brother every day? You think that I'll ever forget the day you drove past my house, followed me and Junito through the alley and waited while Clemenceau killed my brother?" I'm crying too, even though I'm pissed.

"Well, thanks to you, Clem is in the prison hospital right now. Not sure he's gonna make it. Your brother killed Gaston. My mother goes to bury him in Haiti, comes back to find her other son in jail. Because of the Diablos, half of my family is gone. Done. Wiped out."

"It wasn't me." My chest tightens because technically it was. Guilty by association.

The train is long gone and all that's left is the sound of us exhaling, flashing lights, and sirens up ahead.

Do tears make noise? Because I swear I can hear hers falling one at a time.

There's a swirling inside my head. I sit up and feel the earth spin on its axis, and my legs refuse to cooperate.

I look over at her and see blood dripping from a gash in her head. A gash I created. She lies there helplessly. My world is still spinning, but I can move, even if it's only a little bit. We're both seriously hurt. If we wait any longer out here near the train tracks in the cold, we won't make it.

"Come on. We need help." I gaze at the red-and-blue at the top of the hill, in disbelief that I'm actually looking for the police.

I reach for Amy, but she refuses my hand.

"I'm not going to jail. Not when you're the one who stepped to me first. Now let's go. We'll make something up when they ask what happened. Attack dogs on the loose. Train hit us and kept it moving. Take your pick." I'm getting pissed now.

"You go get us help," Amy whispers. "I'll wait here."

My legs feel weak as I beg them to give me the strength to stand. But slowly, they find a will to get me up the hill, the lights growing closer and closer. The crowd parts a bit when they see me.

Stares and whispers.

The stars in my head return. I shake it to make sure

I'm seeing what I'm seeing. DQ and Julicza bent over the hood of DQ's car, hands behind their backs, shackled like criminals.

I want to scream and ask what's going on, but I instead take in the moment. That could be me right now, handcuffed against a car. And where would that leave me? Leave Mami? This is not what Junito wanted. I was supposed to keep the Diablos going. And shut down the Macoutes. But here I am looking to get help for one of them.

I failed.

A bolt of lightning blasts in the sky, and I swear it's almost like Junito sends me a message: *No, you haven't.*

Rain comes down softly. The crowd parts some more.

A trickle of blood runs down the open wound in my forehead, landing in my mouth.

"Somebody help her!" a voice finally screams, getting one of the police officers' attention.

I lock eyes with DQ, face pressed against the hood. His eyes scan the bloody, beaten parts of me. I'm not sure if it was my face that said it or my actual mouth, but the last thing I remember is saying to him, *I'm done.*

And then my knees crash to the ground.

Two arrested in Grafton drug bust

NEWARK, New Jersey
By: Keesha Lester

Officials have announced the arrests of 19-year-old Denny "DQ" Vasquez and one unnamed female minor whom police labeled "street-level dope dealers" in the Grafton Projects area of Newark. Police seized Vasquez's vehicle along with a significant amount of a newly popular strain of marijuana and cocaine with a street value of $1.5 million.

It is rumored that Vasquez was the leader of the local gang the Latin Diablos. On April 13, former alleged leader Juan "Junito" Mendez was gunned down after tensions rose between the Diablos and rival Haitian gang, the Macoutes.

Earlier this year, Clemenceau Mondesir, alleged Macoute leader, and nine other gang members pleaded "no contest" to drug and weapons possession, with an additional murder charge for Mondesir. Three remaining Macoute members waived their right to a trial, taking a plea of twelve years. They have since been transferred from Essex County Jail to Rahway State Prison, while the rest await trial.

Mondesir was recently attacked in jail, allegedly by members of the Diablos, which police believe was ordered by Vasquez. Mondesir's condition has recently been upgraded from serious to stable.

Vasquez will make an initial appearance in court after the Christmas holiday and could face up to 10 years in federal prison and a fine upwards of $10,000. The unnamed minor will appear in juvenile court and will likely face lesser charges.

FELIZ NAVIDAD

HOSPITALS SMELL LIKE ASS. Fried on a hot stone. If I were fully awake, I'd probably say that out loud. But apparently there's a tube in my mouth, and here I am strapped in a hospital bed. Two hospital visits in one year? I've had enough to last me a lifetime.

The lights are too bright and everything is white: the walls, the windows, the snow falling outside. I see a shadowy face popping in and out of my half-closed eyes. Smell the Jean Naté perfume and hear the clank of pearls. Mami.

"She's waking up."

That voice. My heart wants to leap and do pirouettes when I hear Mami speak a full sentence. It is like the greatest gift.

"Feliz navidad, mi'ja." Mami smiles, her face hovering over mine. And another guy. Nametag says Dr. Burrowes. Big beak of a nose. Enough hair in each nostril to make two French braids.

"Where's Amy?" The words muffle through the tube.

Mami looks at Dr. Burrowes, confusion setting in.

"Don't worry, Mrs. Mendez. Incoherent speech can be a common side effect of pain medication."

I'm not hallucinating, pendejo! Did you guys get Amy?

I want to rip the tube from my mouth, spill out the thoughts trapped inside my head. But my eyes have other plans. Closing in *five, four, three . . .*

Two. I see the dancing white lights.

One.

I'm left with only the sound of their words.

"Our scans don't show any signs of brain swelling, which is promising. We would like to keep her here for another couple of days but you'll be able to take her home before the New Year." That's the doctor.

"Dancing?" There is pain and hope in Mami's voice. "Will she dance again?"

"Oh, I'm confident this won't hinder her physically. In fact, dancing is good exercise. I bet she'll be back on the dance floor in no time."

I hear the doctor's footsteps trail to the hallway, the slam of the door closing.

Mami squeezes my hand, showering it with a thousand kisses. "Okay, mi princesa. Now, you fight!"

All my senses have whittled down to two. I feel the warmth of Mami's touch. Hear a knock and a voice at the door.

"Mrs. Mendez, it's Nasser, Beatriz's friend. May I come in?"

Track Five: Dance of the Rumba, December 8, 1983

It's when sleep comes that I am reminded again of who I once was. As always, it takes shape in the form of a dance. Tonight's style? La rumba. Intense, slow, a movement of love, born in Cuba from African slaves, with rhythms so intoxicating they floated across the Caribbean Sea. This was how my old dance teacher, Ms. Maria, once defined it.

I arrive at the bodega early from school. As soon as I open the door, I hear the music with a heavy, accented beat, and a request from Mami: "Beatriz, grab a box of Coke cans from the basement. The soda display is almost empty!"

I take my shoes off and venture down the dark, winding steps as the music floats along with me. The conga drum vibrates. An unfamiliar noise blends in with the rhythm. Heavy breathing. A pendulum of exhales and inhales. Enough to slow my feet as I inch toward the source of the sound and pry open the storage-room door. Darkness and a wall of boxes cover me, with only a pocket of sun peeking through the basement window. And then I see Junito and TJ in the dimness. Two mouths entangled.

I want to scream out, Stop! What are you doing?

But I don't find my voice.

I had seen Junito step to plenty of high-school girls, especially Diablas. Treated them like they meant nothing. Recycled girls like Nixida with the change of each month. But this is different. There is a pile of covers in the middle of the floor. Candles lit, flickering shadows on their faces. I can see the longing, even in their closed eyes.

Junito brushes his hand across TJ's cheek.

"I'm tired of hiding, Juni. Let's just get out of here after the

holidays. Start a new life in San Francisco like we planned." TJ whispers loud enough that I can hear.

"I'll figure something out, but now it's not the right time. Just wait a little longer."

An explosion builds inside of me. Memories of home. The reason why we left. My constant wonder about how it would've been different. I always thought that if Junito had changed—tried harder not to be different—the broken pieces of my family might've been glued back together. And after all we've been through, now Junito has the nerve to consider leaving me and Mami behind? But as I stand there, I realize something. What if it had been Papi who changed? What if he had loved Junito as his true self?

My teeth clench against my inner cheek, the blade pricking me, and I swallow a drop of blood. And I don't care because in this moment I want to rip the sky apart over and over again. My mind tells me to not follow through with the storm I am about to create.

But I don't listen. Something comes over me. It is this very secret that drove us out of Puerto Rico. And it'll be the same secret that'll ruin the new lives we've built in Newark. I can't have that. Not when the Diablo cash flow keeps the Mendezes on top of the world. Not when I am the flyest girl at King Middle School, the princesa that all the girls hope to look like, dress like, be like. So I make a promise to myself right then and there. Someone needs to let Junito know that being with TJ is a threat. And that someone is me.

I remain hidden, counting one, two, three, four, five . . . until I've reached one hundred. They do not hear me, do not see me hidden behind the boxes. But I stare at TJ buttoning his shirt. And I notice a look in Junito's eyes that warns TJ to keep his mouth shut, the promise from his lips that they can continue only in the shadows. TJ blows out the candles and makes his way out the back door, where no one will see him slip through the alley as if that kiss and this moment never happened. He leaves Junito seated on the concrete floor, back pressed against the wall.

I take a step forward. Hear Junito take in a deep breath and hold it in. Two steps. Hear him shuffle to his feet. Three steps. See the weapon pointed in my direction.

"Who's that?" he asks.

Finally I step into the patch of light coming from the small basement window. He lowers his gun and exhales relief as soon as he sees me.

"You're playing with fire, Junito," I warn him.

"Shouldn't you be at school? How long have you been down here?" He throws on his shirt.

"Long enough." I cut my eyes at Junito, but he refuses to look at me. How is it possible to love and hate someone equally? And at what point does one outweigh the other?

Junito finally looks at me as though he hears every word trapped inside my brain.

"I can't help who I am, Beatriz." Both hands are pulling at his face.

"And what will you do when he tells everyone and the whole hood finds out, especially the Diablos?" I fold my arms.

"TJ wouldn't do that."

I laugh out a good, hearty one. "That's not what his cousin told me. The boy's got plans for you." The lie comes out easy.

"You mean Vanessa? She said that?"

I don't say yes. I let my face do that for me. Junito paces the room, smacking the gun against his head.

"Yo, I can't let that happen!"

"Then I think you know what you have to do."

The sun fades into the moon as Junito gathers up the crew to come up with a plan for tomorrow. They'll meet TJ at the top of the hill, choke him up as soon as he steps foot off the bus, gather everyone around to put him on display. Force him into silence with their iron fists and their threats.

A fast-forward jump in my dream. Now replaying the hit on TJ in my mind, my heart cracking, knowing that sometimes even the best plans don't go right. Vanessa Martin—TJ's cousin, my once-upon-a-time friend—wasn't supposed to be there. But when she showed up, I had to do what I knew best, so I let my fists do the talking.

I betrayed all three of them—Junito, TJ, and Vanessa. I feel it all in my sleep: the shock, once again, that Junito's gone. The reality that I was no better than Papi for keeping Junito from being his true self.

My eyes burst open. I see the hospital machines, tubes clinging to me. Abuela clutching her rosary, whispering a prayer. Nasser snoring in the corner chair. Why is he here? How did he find out?

"Dime qué pasó, mi'ja." Mami hovers over me.

"I just had a bad dream . . . sobre el pasado," I say.

Mami brushes one smooth hand across my face. "Don't think about the past. Yesterday is who you once were. Today is who you become."

PROMISES

THERE'S NOTHING BETTER than the sight of Branch Brook Park in late January. Equal parts magic and mystery. How the cherry-tree branches stay strong under the weight of heavy snow gets me every single time. Speaking of time, I been sitting on this bench for the past half hour, maybe longer. Staring at the snow all around, the frozen lake stretched in front of me, the cars riding by. Cars in every color except the yellow I'd hoped would show up.

I should've expected this. I called. No answer. Called again.

Nasser has a job now, Ayita.

And again.

Nasser is at Rutgers for "that program."

In other words, Nasser is everywhere but with me.

The letter I left in his locker yesterday was my final attempt. Maybe pouring myself on the page, like Mrs. Arcentales says in poetry class, would be enough to make him at least hear me out.

Knowing me, I probably spelled something wrong. Or didn't use big enough words like *pulchritude* and *disintegration*. Maybe the voice inside me has been right all along: a girl like me with a boy like that was never meant to be.

I don't know why I showed up with my hair in a bun, wearing lip gloss and a skirt in this freezing-behind weather. Like I'd have some kind of Cinderella moment with Nasser. Shoulda been grateful that he came to see me at the hospital, even though I was too out of it to have an actual conversation.

I keep one eye on the setting sun, knowing that I'll have to head home soon. With the other eye, I stare through the snowy trees ahead. Feet tapping, fingers twitching, like I'm impatiently waiting for the second coming of Jesús.

But nothing. Seconds turn to minutes as the sky changes from orange to pink to medium blue.

A crunch in the snow sounds off behind me. Footsteps. A familiar stab of panic arises as I turn to face the sound.

"It's just me," Nasser says, hands held up in surrender.

What I would give to run and crash myself into the space between those hands. Would Nasser hold me back? Or would he tell me we can try again?

I sip in a quick, icy breath, stand up, and move in for a hug. And then Nasser does the absolute worst thing. He taps me on my shoulder—twice—like I'm his homeboy.

"I didn't think you were coming." I'm barely able to hide the disappointment in my voice.

No answer. Just eyes forward. Gloveless hands shoved in his pockets.

"I finally went back to school this week. Mami didn't care that the doctors said I could return earlier. She kept me held hostage at home."

Silence.

"Got my teeth fixed." I flash my new pearly smile, courtesy of the dentist. "The scars are starting to heal. Abuela put Vivaporu all over my face. That woman swears it's a cure-all."

I laugh. He doesn't.

"That was sweet of you to show up at the hospital like that. Abuela told me how she called your house, looking for me. She got nervous when she saw the cops outside."

A hard swallow, followed by a hard stare with those eyes of his.

"I've spoken to your mom a lot. Heard you got a job, and you got accepted into that college prep class. That's why I haven't seen you around school much?"

A nod. I'll take it.

"Gonna start choreography for ACT-SO with Señorita Amaro next week. Will you be at dance class?"

A shake of his head, and my whole spirit sinks.

"How long we gonna play this game, Nasser? I'm so sorry for how things left off. But I'm different. Better. Got my report card. It's the best I've ever seen it. Got you to thank for that. And I'm gonna start training for ACT-SO. Things are looking up."

Nasser exhales so hard it sounds like it hurts. "Are you still a Diabla?"

I don't answer him. Instead I say, "I miss you."

I take a step forward. He takes a step back. I try again with, "I miss us."

"You're avoiding my question, Beatriz."

"Why does it matter? There's too much going on with what they're saying in the papers, and with DQ and Julicza gone, we're not even meeting anymore. I plan on quitting. It's just hard because they're my friends, you know?"

Nasser pulls one hand out of his pocket to look at his watch. Time is the enemy.

"I should get going. I just wanted to check on you. See how you're doing. And give this back," he says.

He flips his hand to reveal the folded-up letter, the words I worked so hard to write. He places it right in my palm and the brush of his fingertips seems to shift the season from winter to summer. The letter slips between my open fingers and falls on the ground. The snow wets the ink and like magic, a single line bleeds through: *forgiveness is a gift.*

We both look at the words come to life, but our faces don't show the same reaction.

"We can start over, Nasser. Take things slow. Be friends again?" I turn into one of those ridiculous, begging girls on the telenovelas.

"I'd say you have enough friends, Beatriz Ayita." He grabs both of my hands and squeezes them as if it'll be the last time he'll ever touch me. And then, Nasser Kervin Moreau turns his back to me and trudges through the snow.

The tears come in hot and fast. I want to run after him, grab him by the shoulders, and shake them over and over until every word I say turns to truth in his ears. But I can't move. My feet and my words and my lies won't let me. I haven't followed through with the promise I made to myself. That I'd quit the Diablos as soon as 1985 hit. If I can't keep a promise to myself, what makes me think I can keep a promise to Nasser?

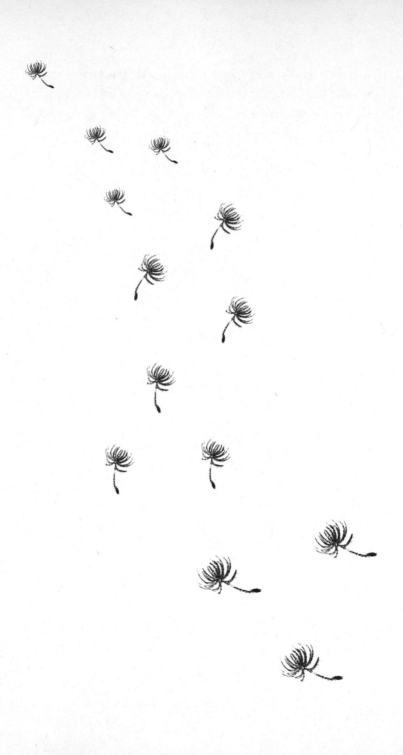

ENCORE: SOARING

MARCH 21, 1985
NAME: BEATRIZ MENDEZ
COURSE: FREEFORM POETRY (ELECTIVE,
MRS. ARCENTALES, THIRD MARKING PERIOD)
ASSIGNMENT: WRITE A POEM ABOUT HEALING.

LONG AGO, MAMI ONCE SAID,
"EL UNIVERSO LO CURA TODO."
THE UNIVERSE HEALS ALL THINGS.
BUT THAT AIN'T ENTIRELY TRUE.
IT'S EL RITMO THAT MENDS THE BROKEN,
THE TIMBALES TAKING THEIR TIME WITH YOU,
SHAKING, STIRRING, SHAPING YOU INTO ALL THAT IS GOOD,
AND SOMETIMES NOT SO GOOD TOO.
THE TAMBOR BUILDS YOUR INSIDES,
STRONG LIKE MOUNTAINS,
FILLING YOU UP WITH LOVE TO DROWN OUT THE HATE,
LIGHT TO BRIGHTEN THE DARK SPACES,
AND THE BAD PARTS . . . LIKE PAIN.
SOMETIMES SO MUCH OF IT THAT YOU'LL QUESTION IF YOU,
AND YOUR DREAMS,
AND THIS LIFE ARE ENOUGH.
AND IN THE END, EVEN WHEN THE RHYTHM
FEELS TOO FAST, TOO HEAVY,
THERE YOU ARE KEEPING UP, BREAKING WALLS,
AND DANCING ANYWAY.

A+ EXCELLENT WORK, BEATRIZ! YOUR WORDS DANCE!
—MRS. ARCENTALES

IF YOU BELIEVE IT, THEN ACT-SO!

MY EYES ARE FIXED on the audience. Center, third row from front. Mami, her hands laced with Mr. Martin's; Abuela and her buddy Ms. Geraldine; Señorita Amaro; Mrs. Ruiz; and Dr. Brown. The rest of the Arts High auditorium is packed with spectators, but I don't zone in on them. I take in the energy of my family, breathe away the memories of yesterday. Papi. The Diablos. All the wrong I've done. Inhale the good coming my way: My exit. My new beginning.

"Contestant number twenty-seven is Beatriz Mendez, representing Barringer High School, performing a Latin-jazz fusion dance to 'Fame'!" The announcer's voice rings out.

This is it. A second chance. To get it right. To see myself transformed. To feel the weight of Debbie Allen's words: "The minute you learn to dance, it becomes yours for life." And right here, as I wait for the stagehand to press play, I am fixed in fourth position, arms extended, ready to live pa' siempre.

The music begins with the strum of a guitar. Three chords in, I am hypnotized, fingers tingling, and I fold my whole body into the rhythm. I swing my red skirt, and each chord spreads like wildfire within me. I glide center stage, the beat picks up—syncopated, heart-thrumming—and I hear Señorita Amaro cheer from the audience, "Wepaaaa!"

I stamp my foot against the ground, flick my wrists, and clap for four counts. The audience joins in with me. Four pirouette turns, my eyes zoom in on one spot, way in the back of the auditorium by the double doors. That's when I see him.

White shirt. Collar flipped. Dark pants. Smile gleaming.

Nasser "The Victorious One" Moreau. Señor Sabe'todo. Mr. Arm & Hammer himself.

He came.

The electric guitar intensifies right along with Irene Cara's powerful voice. And that's when I lose it, heart beating like a caged bird begging to be set free. In my mind I hear Señorita Amaro's commands: *Pirouette! Three, two, four, two! Chassé lift! And one, two, two, two!* I dance through every move and watch the world around me disappear.

Halfway through the song, the beat mixes with the sounds of the wooden clave and the conga drum, keeping the lyrics of "Fame" but adding in a salsa twist. This remixed style of music is new to the scene, and just as Señorita Amaro predicted, the audience goes loco!

The applause fills me up, readies me for a flying leap, and when I do, my feet climb the ladder to the sky. Tension fills the air, tries its best to take over, to challenge my will to finish. But I won't let it win. I push through, four counts to go. Last possé turn, last arabesque, and the music ends.

Silence. All I can hear is breath, and all I can see are eyes. I exhale loudly and let out a rousing, "Wepa!"

The applause earthquakes through the auditorium. Everyone is shouting something different. "Bravo!" "That was fresh to death!" "She killed it!" I take a bow and try my best not to cry.

Right there, even though we are inside Arts High School on a Saturday spring afternoon, I feel the stars fill up the sky. It took three months after the incident with Amy to get back to this point. Dancing as though my life depended on it, and though it took some time to realize it, I knew it was true. I have finally become me ... Beatriz. The real me ... that I was always meant to be.

I look out into the audience, see the sea of people up on their feet. See my special cheer section, smack in the middle. If love were a color, it'd be rainbow—a radiant arc after a storm.

But when I check, I see that Nasser is gone. Not every rainbow is perfect, I guess.

The curtains close, just in time to hide my smile that is fading fast.

The sound guy hands me my tape and says, "Good job." I'm sure I don't even answer him back.

I walk farther backstage, past the other contestants, smiling, whispering, congratulating me. But none of it matters. What I felt a minute ago when I saw Nasser made the whole earth stop. And even though he didn't stay, he saw me in my rawest form.

I find my dance bag lined up against the wall in the hallway beside the auditorium. As soon as I bend over to grab it, I hear the clack of hard shoes. See the shiny penny loafers strolling my way. And when I stand all the way up, he's already here. In my face. Smiling.

"That was amazing, Beatriz."

I feel stars burst beneath my feet, if there ever was such a thing.

"Thank you. I didn't think I'd see you in the audience. Did you compete yet?"

"Sure did. Recited my poem for the judges in the art room, right before you went onstage." He grins.

We stand there, silence lingering between us. Seconds pass. Our hands become magnets. Two months. That's how long it's been. Two months of barely seeing each other at school. Barely speaking. Just a "hello" here and a "have a nice day" there in between bell rings on the days he did have class at Barringer. Once, maybe twice a week. Two months since the last time I felt his touch.

"I've missed you," I say. My hands clench his shirt, pulling him forward, praying he doesn't pull back like last time.

He doesn't.

"Missed you too, Beatriz. I didn't think I would. But I do."

Those lips hover a few inches above mine, waiting for me to stand on my tippy toes to reach them. And I swear it's just like a scene out of a telenovela, where the violins come in all romantic and junk and the trumpets scream, the door busts open, and the whole familia ruins the moment.

Because that's exactly what happens next.

"¡Dios mío, qué talento!" It's Abuela's show now, with her fast feet and her big voice echoing down the hallway.

My whole entire crew is scurrying behind her in order to keep up.

"I'm so proud, mi'ja." Mami hands me a bouquet of tulips soon as she reaches me.

More hugs. More compliments. From everybody. Even Mr. Stoneface Martin himself.

In a perfect world, this should be a Polaroid picture. A complete circle, with me standing in the middle, surrounded by pieces of a puzzle that, from the outside, look like they wouldn't fit. But somehow they do. And oddly enough, there's not a Diablo anywhere.

"Guys, I'd like to introduce you to—" I start.

"Nasser, amorcito lindo!" Abuela interrupts me, screaming.

And the Academy Award goes to Abuela. Except this performance seems real as hell. Nasser's eating it up too, hugging her back. Like him and her been homies forever.

Mami steps in. "We got to know your friend very well at the hospital."

Dr. Brown reaches through the crowded huddle to shake Nasser's and my hand. "Well, you've certainly made Barringer proud, Beatriz. You too, young man. I was able to catch your performance right before Beatriz's. Great job on your poem." Then he zips up his jacket.

"Where are you going, Dr. Brown?" Nasser asks.

"Yeah, you should stick around for the awards. I mean, I'm not sure if I'll win," I say.

Mami slaps me on the shoulder. "Don't talk like that!"

"Well, I don't know if my poem will get anything either," Nasser says.

Mami gives him a whack too.

Dr. Brown checks his watch. "I have to head home. But when you two get to school on Monday, be sure to stop by my office to show me your medals."

He winks at us both and walks down the hall, past the auditorium, and straight out the exit doors.

Doing Barringer proud: Freshman and junior students headed to ACT-SO nationals

NEWARK, New Jersey
By: Keesha Lester

Beatriz Mendez sounds more like a political candidate than a dance competitor.

"I didn't find dance. Dance found me. It gave me a chance for a better future. I hope that young children will see me and be inspired to find their own passion in life."

Fifteen-year-old Beatriz Mendez didn't have it easy growing up. Upon her arrival in Newark from Puerto Rico at the age of eight, language barriers prevented her from excelling in school. That has changed since she's entered Barringer High School, where she is involved in peer tutoring and a new freeform poetry class. Last year she witnessed the death of her brother, Juan "Junito" Mendez, alleged leader of the Latin Diablo gang. Some eight months later, Ms. Mendez was hospitalized as a result of an attack but was unable to identify her assailant. Authorities have not been able to confirm if the incident was isolated or connected to the now-defunct Haitian Macoute gang.

Nasser Moreau came from humble beginnings, born in the coastal town of Léogâne, Haiti. He and his family left Haiti during the Duvalier era of extreme political turmoil. Shortly after, they settled in Miami, Florida. There, Moreau flourished academically and artistically. He speaks four languages—"Really, three and a half," he explains—and enjoys writing poetry and playing the guitar. Moreau is new to Barringer this year and is already soaring his way to the top of his class.

Despite Mendez's and Moreau's hardships, theirs has a fairy-tale ending.

A freshman and junior, respectively, at Barringer High School, they are heading to the national ACT-SO Competition in Dallas, Texas. The competition is the brainchild of journalist Vernon Jarrett, who wanted to create an "Olympics of the Mind" for youth of African descent in America.

This will be their first time competing in an event of this caliber. They won gold medals in the dance and poetry categories of the local competition, joining three other gold medalists from Arts and University High Schools in the science, math, and vocal categories. Stay tuned for articles about the other winners.

McDonald's Restaurant Corporation and the Urban League will cover the winners' expenses to the national competition. Scheduled to appear as celebrity judges for this summer's event are Jennifer Holliday, Tony Award–winning star of the Broadway musical "Dreamgirls"; Alice Walker, Pulitzer Prize–winning author of "The Color Purple"; and Debbie Allen, Emmy Award–winning choreographer and star of "Fame."

We have no doubt that Mendez and Moreau will compete well and bring national gold medals back to Barringer High!

ANOTHER YEAR, ANOTHER SHOT

I NEVER THOUGHT I'D spend my fifteenth birthday staring down the barrel of a gun, let alone hearing the sound of a single shot that killed my brother. I didn't expect to spend the time after his death living for him, for his purpose and not my own. I never really chose to become a Diabla, selling poison in the streets and in my school. The dance floor was my calling—the passion that was sealed for me long ago when I used to dance on the sandy beaches of Puerto Rico.

It's been almost a year without Junito. Each day has been different. Some beautiful, some more painful. All three of us—Mami, Abuela, and me—have spent days and nights, in our own way, crying for him to come back, until there were no tears left. We lost count of how often the sun turned to moon and the moon became sun, and we yelled at God for doing what comes naturally—taking life away to begin fresh. It took some time for the three of us to realize that what we have now is what we had all along: strength, unity, amor.

I am silent as I kneel at the altar between Mami and Abuela. All three of us dressed as if we're going somewhere fancy—Mami's request. I knew better than to fight back when she handed me a blue velvet swing dress and a red rose for my hair.

Today is not about me. This is for Junito.

Abuela clutches her rosary, whispering Spanish prayers of peace on this one-year anniversary of the shooting. I glance at Mami as if I'm waiting for her to relapse, for her voice to shut off like a light switch, like it did when the doctors broke the news. I also wait for tears. The rushing rivers that I haven't seen fall from her eyes in months. Perhaps the tears have been relieved by my return to dancing, or her running the bodega again, or the poetry styles I share with her from my new class at school, even though she refuses to follow the rules. ¿Quién necesita las reglas cuando tienes corazón?

And while I'd like to think that I've found my healing in dance, I'm sure that Mami has found hers in those beautiful, speak-worthy, rule-breaking words she records in her journal.

Mami turns to today's latest poem. A Spanish haiku of sorts that she wrote as she sat outside the bodega when the sun rose. She tapes it to the wall next to a picture of Junito's smiling face.

> *Tu ausencia*
> *es temporal mi hi'jo*
> *tu amor . . . es eterno*

This simple poem, breaking the haiku pattern, is probably her best one yet. I translate it in my head into English.

Your absence is temporary, my son; your love is eternal. I repeat the poem aloud in Spanish, counting the off-beats in a whisper, praying Junito hears and feels every single word.

Mami leans over the altar and blows out the candles.

"¡Ven, Beatriz! I have a surprise for you," Mami says.

She reaches for my hand to lift me off the floor, and then I do the same for Abuela.

"What's going on?" I ask, looking at Abuela for an answer, but all she does is laugh and say, "Yo no sé nada."

Together we walk down the stairs. Me in the middle, one hand clutched to Mami and one to Abuela like an unbreakable chain. Mami opens the door and the sun pours in, almost blinding my view of Nasser standing there, holding three single, wrapped roses. Two yellow. One red.

"Happy birthday, Beatriz *Ayita*," he says, handing the yellow roses to Mami and Abuela and the red one to me.

My stomach pulls and tugs in every direction.

"¡Amorcito, qué bello!" Abuela doesn't even give me a chance to say anything to Nasser. She can't stop herself from squeezing his cheeks, telling him how handsome he looks in his khaki pants, bow tie, and grown-man shoes.

Mami grabs me by the shoulders and commands, "Go out and enjoy!"

That stomach thing starts up again, and I know exactly why. "I can't leave you alone. Not today of all days."

Mami looks at me with hopeful eyes. "You turn sixteen only one time, mi'ja. Today we all get out of the house. Abuela and I have plans too. Come back and we have cake and sing. Together, como una familia."

"Okay, I'll be back by nine. And there's something I need to do tonight."

Mami gazes deep into my eyes, like she knows.

Abuela winks at me. "Now, he take you to dinner."

"El carro te espera," Nasser says, pointing to the taxi.

That sends Mami leaping a bit, her yellow rose still pressed close to her chest. "¡Ay! He's learning Spanish so nicely, Beatriz!"

"Words are his thing, Mami. I'm sure he'll master it soon and move on to German by next week."

"Hey, that's not a bad idea!" Nasser lifts a finger to his temple.

He escorts me to the car and opens the door for me. Mr. Martin's car pulls up right behind Nasser's taxi.

I wave at Mr. Martin, and when he waves back, I don't know why, but it sends my hopes soaring.

Nasser and I pull off down Broadway, with the cool spring breeze sifting through the crack in the window. We zoom down the Garden State Parkway, far away from our world in Newark, and get off the exit for Clark.

Clark is a suburb. The chances of seeing Bigfoot outweigh the possibility of seeing any black or brown faces roaming these streets. When we pull into a restaurant parking lot, I just about drop my mouth on the floor. Nasser Kervin Moreau is taking me on a real date, to a real fancy joint. Friendly's. There's waiters and tables where they come up to us and ask us what we want to order.

"What will you have to eat, young man?" The waitress speaks to Nasser first.

"I'll have the steak with fries."

"And how would you like your steak cooked?"

"Medium well."

"And for the lady?"

"Don't be shy, Beatriz. Order whatever you want. It's her birthday," he tells the waitress. She announces it to the whole restaurant and everyone starts clapping.

I order the chicken salad, chicken and broccoli cheese pasta, and a Coke with lemon.

"I'm not sure what I did," I tell Nasser.

"Did for what?"

"To deserve you." I move my hair to cover my face.

"You don't have to do that. You're beautiful just the way you are." Nasser sticks my hair behind my ear. I leave it right there where it belongs.

Dinner is delicious and when we're done with it, the staff brings out a brownie sundae with a candle lit, and they sing "Happy Birthday" to me. After dinner Nasser drives me to this beautiful park called Warinanco in Roselle. The sun is falling just as we arrive. We take a walk around the lake, throwing pieces of Nasser's leftover fries to all the ducks. Finally we settle on a big rock near the weeping willow trees beside the lake, where we talk about our lives until we chase the sun from the sky. His stories, my stories intertwining, like tracks on a mixtape playing on repeat.

"Speaking of music, I have a surprise for you," he says.

Nasser takes his guitar out of its case and positions the strap around his shoulder. He strums the guitar and two chords in, I already know.

"You learned how to play my song?"

Señorita Amaro has been teaching me a new dance for the ACT-SO national contest: "Out Here On My Own."

I love this Irene Cara joint from the *Fame* movie.

"Dance for me," Nasser says, so smooth, so sweet, I just about lose it.

He plays and with each chord, I begin to move like nothing else matters. Knees close together for a perfect backswing, careful of my lines, just like Señorita Amaro taught me. I try my best to remain poised through each movement, press down the excitement that's been building inside ever since I saw that newspaper article.

In a few months I will dance for Debbie Allen.

Once upon a time, I really did wonder who I was, where I fit in. But not anymore. Nothing and no one will take away my chance. These days, the inhala, exhala feels easier.

Especially since I know what's coming next. Tonight's the night.

Nasser and I play and dance to his guitar version of the song until the moon takes its place in the sky.

As he strums the last chord, I take a bow, envisioning the hundreds of people in the audience at nationals. I want to stay right beneath the moon, beside this lake, wrapped into arms where I finally feel free.

A soft kiss on my forehead breaks me out of my vision.

"I'm not going to leave you. We can do this together," Nasser whispers in my ear.

We'd talked about how this would play out again and again. He begged, bargained, pleaded, but I stayed true.

Some burdens are meant to be carried alone.

We head back to the taxi and cruise back up the Parkway, his one hand on the steering wheel, the other gripping me tight as though the pressure is enough to change my mind. We take the long way through the winding Branch Brook roads lined with cherry blossoms, past the bright lights that line Route 21, until we reach the front of the bodega.

Nasser puts the car in park. "Let's get this over with once and for all."

"No, I got this." I graze my fingers across Nasser's face. It stops him from taking off his seatbelt.

"Will you be okay?" he asks.

"I'll be just fine."

He cracks his knuckles. "And if something happens . . ."

"You'll be the first person I call."

And with that promise, I kiss him good night, sneak past Geraldine, slip to the basement unseen, prop open the back door, and wait. The wait's not long. Soon everyone shows up.

Track Six: Dance of La Salsa, 1974 (A Wish)

Later that night, I'm exhausted. Sleep comes fast and it brings a new dream. A new track.

We are back where we started. Right in the barrio, in front of our casita in Aguadilla, playing with our cousins. Mami and Abuela are pinning up wet clothes on the laundry line, where they will bake under the Caribbean sun and dance in the afternoon wind. We sing our song while jumping rope. Junito is with us, laughing, carefree and singing, bouncing to the rhythm.

Papi pulls up in a car with our tíos. He is not drunk. Not an ounce of alcohol on his breath. He jumps in the rope and sings along with us.

Mi madre y mi padre
viven en la calle
de San Valentín
número cuarenta y ocho.

Our voices fold into each other as we sing a sweet song about where our parents live. And when Papi's brothers start to make fun of Junito—the fact that he doesn't play with the other boys in the barrio, but instead chooses to jump rope with his primas and hermana—Papi does not care for one second.

"Leave my boy alone. He's perfect the way God made him."

Suddenly my heart explodes with the heat of a million suns.

The sky darkens a bit just as Mami finishes cooking dinner. She props the radio on the windowsill and turns up the volume when "Indestructible" by Ray Barretto comes on. The wooden claves take over, dominating our hands, hips, feet, and heart. Papi, my cousins, my uncles, Junito, and the whole barrio begin to move. Fingers clasped, spinning with the earth, melting into the magic that is la música salsa. The lyrics bleed true: when you go through a hard time in life, in that moment . . . take fate into your own hands. And that's exactly what we Mendezes will do. We'll be indestructible, together.

The song ends and Mami calls us inside, where we will feast on tonight's spread: pork chops, rice and beans, and tostones, of course. Junito holds my hand as we walk inside, and he whispers to me, "I'm okay now. We're okay. I can be who I want to be. And I want you to do the same."

I turn over in my sleep. My every dream from this night will be filled with sweet thoughts like this, even if they are a figment of my imagination.

TAKING FLIGHT—
THREE MONTHS LATER

AFTER MY BIRTHDAY NIGHT in the park with Nasser, I waited down here in the storage room of the basement. Held one final meeting. They all showed up too, even with DQ gone. I looked every single Diablo in the eye. Told them I was done. I didn't care about the money, wearing the flyest gear, how my family would get by. We'd known rock bottom before. We'd come out of this better, stronger, *indestructible*.

I waited for a reaction. *Blood in, blood out*, right? Those were the rules. But one by one, every single Diablo walked out of the room, a series of whispers trailing behind them.

"Better watch your back, princesa."

"We don't need you. We'll do our own thing."

And finally a squeeze of a hand and the softest whisper of all: "I get it. Happy birthday, though."

That was the last time Maricela and I spoke.

And I swear I heard Abuela in my head that night in both Spanish and English: A veces se pierde amigos en el camino al éxito. Sometimes we lose friends on the path to success.

Not one Diablo touched me that night or anytime since, and I knew that had everything to do with Junito. My guardian angel still looked over me, people still loved and feared and respected him, even from the grave.

I didn't quit the Diablos because I stopped loving Junito. It's because the longer I hung on, the more I realized that I was losing the love I once had for myself.

My time as a dealer is over. I had enough of seeing it, knowing how it affected the people of my city. Walking away was the only way to discover who I was meant to become: Beatriz Mendez, NAACP ACT-SO gold medalist, fourth marking period "Most Improved" freshman at Barringer High School, future dancer headed for fame.

I haven't seen or heard from Amy since all those months ago when we fought on the train tracks. I sent help but when cops searched the scene, all they found was a blonde wig, a Polaroid camera, and a picture of me running, looking scared as hell.

Sometimes I wonder where Amy is, where she went that night, and how she's living now. Did she eventually go back to Haiti? Is the emptiness still there? 'Cause sometimes it's still in me too. Living and growing, though, I've found a way to rise above it. In a lot of ways, we are alike. Caught between two worlds, trying to find a way to prove ourselves and make it in a new place, even though memories of our islands, both sweet and bitter, are still ingrained in our minds. Feet planted here, hearts left behind in the Caribbean. We both lost brothers. I'm glad she didn't lose both of hers, actually. And now we have to learn how to become and how to overcome all at once.

I take a look around the storage room, the space Junito called his own. All the while, this place was nothing more than a representation of his own battles. Dedicated to building a gang of people he could call family as a way of replacing the love he never got from Papi. But that room was also his escape. A place where he and TJ could be together without the world looking down and frowning. I messed that up. With my fears and my lies, Junito beat TJ up for all of Grafton and Broadway to see. To prove that he was exactly who Papi wanted him to be . . . un hombre fuerte. But in the end, that only made things worse.

The reality sinks in that this space is for only me now—my dreams, my dancing, my way out. The posters of Diablo gang symbols are gone. All the red decorations, adios. All that is left behind is my graffiti tag: ¡Fama! Quiero vivir pa' siempre! This room is now a dance studio where my hands, feet, and corazón will create movements that will live forever. After I won ACT-SO, Mami, Ms. Geraldine, and I installed a wall of mirrors and a barre for me to do stretches. There's a table in the corner with a big boom box and lots of tapes filled with salsa, bomba, rap, pop, and R&B. My walls are covered in posters of my favorite stars of *Fame*. Especially Debbie Allen.

Next to the table there's a garbage can with only one thing in it. Yesterday's *Newark Ledger*, complete with the headline: "September trial set for murder of Newark gang leader."

"Beatriz, gotta get to the airport. ¡Están aquí!" Mami yells down the basement steps.

"Coming, Mami!" I turn off the lights inside my dance studio.

When I get to the door outside the bodega, Mami and Abuela are talking with Señorita Amaro, our chaperone for the trip. Nasser winks at me and places my suitcase in the trunk of the taxi. His dad is taking us to Newark airport. We're heading to Dallas early for rehearsals and historic tours planned for the contestants. Our families will meet us out there in two days.

"This is it." Mami kisses my forehead, pulls me in close. I drown myself in her embrace.

"Thank you, Mami. For everything."

"No, no. Gracias, Beatriz."

"You'll be okay while I'm gone?" I ask.

Mr. Martin pulls up in his Chevrolet Celebrity.

"Sweetie, not only will I be fine, we both will live now . . . for us." She smiles real wide. When Mr. Martin gets out of the car, she runs over to him and plants a kiss on his cheek.

Then I see TJ. I can spot that 'fro a mile away. I often thought about what would happen when this day came. And here we are. He gets out of Mr. Martin's car and walks toward me, and my hands turn clammy.

"Hey . . . TJ." My voice is hesitant. "I didn't know you were back from San Francisco."

"Just flew in this morning. I got me a summer internship in New York. Uncle Daniel's taking your mom out to dinner at Je's downtown, and they invited me to come along."

I swallow hard at the thought of that. In a perfect world, Junito would be going with him.

"Well, I just wanted to say hi, Beatriz. Good seeing you."

I wonder if he's lying.

"TJ!" I call out as he starts to walk away. "You ever wonder if one day you could . . ."

"Forgive you?" He turns to face me.

I chew on my bottom lip and nod slowly.

"Already did that a long time ago." TJ stands there, giving me the once-over, probably wondering what more I have to add.

"Actually, I forgive *both* of you." As soon as he says that, I feel my knees buckle a bit.

TJ reaches for my hands.

"I miss him so bad." My voice breaks midsentence.

"I've got some good memories to hold on to. Dig deep, Beatriz, and find those moments too." He gives my hands a firm squeeze and heads toward Mr. Martin's car.

"Will you still be here when I get back?" I shout out to TJ, tears welling up in my eyes.

"All summer long. So will Vanessa."

I smile at that, knowing I still might have a chance to make things right. Mr. Moreau turns the key in the ignition as I hop in the back seat of his taxi. Then he busts a U-turn in the middle of Broadway, blasting "Save Your Love (for #1)" on the radio, and we speed off.

Nasser turns around in the front seat. "Who was that you were talking to?"

"Oh, just my brother's old boyfriend." The words come out with ease.

Nasser nods. He knows what's up now.

Señorita Amaro reaches for my hand as we zip down the highway, windows rolled all the way down, the summer breeze whirling around us. A few wishmaker seeds float in through my window, swaying slowly to the rhythm.

I think back to the memory of Friday the thirteenth—the lonely wishmaker flower I saw, searching for the sun as shots rang through my life. But that was yesterday, and if yesterday is what I once was, then today I'm becoming someone else.

A single seed dances its way to the palm of my hand.

"Make a wish, Beatriz," Señorita Amaro says.

I press my fingers together, close my eyes real tight, see the curtains opening, feel the pulse of the music as Debbie Allen smiles from the judges' table. And then . . . I imagine myself soaring.

AUTHOR'S NOTE

Becoming Beatriz is a work of fiction. That means I got to make some stuff up and you know what? I had a blast doing it.

Now that we've cleared the air, the plot contains some threads that are grounded in personal details of my life. For example, my father lived in the Grafton Projects of Newark. I spent the early part of my childhood there. Like Beatriz, I studied many forms of dance at the Maria Priadka Dance School, I watched *Fame*, and I competed in the NAACP ACT-SO contest in high school.

There are also some threads of history that I think are worth mentioning here.

ABOUT GANGS AND THE DRUG
EPIDEMIC OF THE 1980s

I grew up in Newark, New Jersey, and went to school there all my life, attending Madison Elementary School and University High School. (Go Phoenix!) Yes, Newark is a city, complete with an unfortunate history of drugs and gangs. But let me be very clear: my childhood memories of Newark will forever be sweet. The busted-open fire hydrants in the dead of July; going to the bodega for penny candy; and the mix of salsa, rap, and R&B blasting from corner to corner. Not to mention hearing stories of people who came from my beloved city and went on to claim real fame: Shaquille O'Neal, Whitney Houston, Amiri Baraka, Queen Latifah. The list is endless.

Like any American city, however, Newark sometimes gets a bad rap. The drug epidemic that gripped the city in the early 1980s was well documented in various newspapers. Heroin and cocaine were the drugs of choice, followed by crack cocaine in 1985. Unlike expensive cocaine (about a hundred dollars a gram in the early 80s), crack was cheap, selling for as little as three dollars. Naturally this led to a widespread epidemic in metropolitan areas like Newark. Some of the newspaper articles featured in this novel, though written to serve the plot, were inspired by real *Star-Ledger* articles. Thanks to the wonderful librarians in the Charles F. Cummings New Jersey Information Center at the Newark Public Library, I had a chance to learn how drug problems affected our city.

The Macoutes and Diablos are gangs made from my own imagination. Real gangs, however, existed in Newark in the 1980s and still do today, as they do in other cities across the United States. According to the National Gang Center (www.nationalgangcenter.gov), young people join gangs for many reasons: loss of a parent, financial gains, problems at home, protection, and more. There are hundreds, even thousands, of young people like Beatriz and Junito who have experienced these types of problems. Joining a gang does not have to be the answer.

If you or someone you know is at risk of gang involvement, there are resources and support services that can help. **Contact the National Gang Center at (800) 446-0912.**

In 1976, renowned African American journalist Vernon Jarrett developed his idea of an "Olympics of the Mind" through a contest he named Afro-Academic, Cultural, Technological, and Scientific Olympics (ACT-SO). It's aligned with the NAACP, the National Association for the Advancement of Colored People. Established in 1909, the NAACP is the United States' oldest and largest civil rights organization.

For the sake of the plot, I altered some of the details and timelines. For starters, while the first national ACT-SO contests were held in 1978, only seven cities participated.

Newark was not one of them. The first New Jersey contest was held in 1989, four years after Beatriz won her regional contest. In addition, Nasser performs a poem for his segment of competition. While ACT-SO did include a poetry segment in 1985, it was only in written form. In 2015, spoken poetry was added as a separate competition.

I competed in the local and national contests for ACT-SO between 1994 and 1998. It is an experience that I am extremely grateful to have had in my teen years. It molded me into a public speaker, exposed me to students of various Afro-centric backgrounds from all across the country, and taught me the values of discipline and perseverance. During my competition years, there were students of color from different backgrounds who participated: Black, Hispanic, Asian, and Native American too. (I clearly remember one Filipino violinist who brought the house down with a Beethoven piece!)

The current website for ACT-SO states that the contest is open to African American students, yet a separate page also states that ACT-SO provides a forum for "students of African descent." In writing a story about a girl from Puerto Rico who competes in ACT-SO, I thought it was worth mentioning the complexities and misunderstandings that exist within communities of color.

Beatriz Mendez is what people today would consider Afro-Latina, or Afro-Latinx, where the *x* symbolizes intersecting identities and racial backgrounds that exist within Latin American culture. In other words, Beatriz is both black *and* Puerto Rican. Her race is Black. Her ethnicity is Puerto Rican. Her nationality is American. This type of complex diversity exists within my own family. Come to one Christmas dinner and you'll have a cup of coquito in one hand and a plate of fried chicken and collard greens in the other, while kompa music blasts in the background.

It is my hope that this novel opens up more conversations about diversity within diversity. These types of conversations add to the growing spectrum of stories that show there is no single, authentic lived experience in communities of color. As authors, we are the lucky ones who get to show all this on the page.

ABOUT DEBBIE ALLEN

Some of Debbie Allen's accomplishments are presented in this novel, but it's worth mentioning some key points of her life story here. At the young age of four, Debbie Allen had her future figured out. She wanted to be a professional dancer. But in 1950s Texas, life was hard for people of color. The racial divide that existed in the United States was in fact so deep that Debbie's mother, Vivian Ayers, moved her family to Mexico. As a result, Debbie and her siblings became fluent in Spanish.

At the age of sixteen, Debbie decided to give her

childhood dance dreams a real shot when she auditioned for the North Carolina School of the Performing Arts. She was denied admission because according to the selection committee, she had the wrong body type.

Regardless of early challenges, Debbie Allen went on to fulfill her dance dreams, performing in Broadway shows, starring in *Fame*, singing, composing music, and directing some of entertainment's most iconic television shows and films. As impressive as her work on camera is (I adore her role as Dr. Catherine Avery on *Grey's Anatomy*!), it is Ms. Allen's work off camera that is the most impactful.

On July 8, 2018, I had the opportunity to fulfill my childhood wish of dancing alongside *the* Ms. Lydia Grant—Debbie Allen. And let me tell you, I could not keep up! Ms. Allen graciously gives back to the community by hosting Salsa Sundays at the Wallis Annenberg Center for the Performing Arts in Beverly Hills, California. In 2001, she opened the Debbie Allen Dance Academy, a nonprofit organization for children in kindergarten through twelfth grade. While in California, I had the opportunity to witness young rising stars putting their dreams to work. I saw firsthand the impact that dance can have on a young life. Debbie Allen may have played Lydia Grant on television, but it's her real-life legacy that will last for years to come.

ACKNOWLEDGMENTS

I can't believe I'm writing another round of thank-yous for a book I wrote. Wow! This feeling will never, ever get old.

Let me preface these acknowledgments by saying that if I forgot to mention your name, I'm sorry! I'm sleep deprived, okay? But I love you. Promise.

I give the greatest honor to God! It is my faith in Him that keeps me going.

To my son, Christopher, you are my endless gift. Nasser Charles, the greatest definition of love and friendship, te amo con todo mi corazón. Huge thanks to my parents, Jennifer and Robert Peters, and my brother,

Robert Peters II, for their belief in this dream (and their supreme babysitting skills!).

To Lara Perkins, my literary agent. I'm amazed at how you juggle everything. Wife. Mom. Agent to writers like me who need constant attention. (Ha!) Thank you for this journey.

How far would an editor go to show commitment to character? How about trying to function with a pseudo-blade (actually a piece of sea glass) inside her cheek? That would be my editor, Karen Boss. Karen, you're the real MVP! Thank you for your keen eye, feedback, and patience.

To the entire Charlesbridge team, and especially to Yolanda Scott, Mel Schuit, Donna Spurlock, Rachel Doody, Megan Quinn, Hanna Lafferty, and Joyce White. Also, a huge shout-out to cover illustrator Alyssa Bermudez!

I have the best family and friends a girl could ask for. A beautiful, colorful, multilingual crew of damas, caballeros, and madames whom I am so blessed to call my own. Thank you for reading early drafts and for putting me in check when I needed it: Jaylis Arcentales, Julicza Feliciano, Fallon Dumont-Sajous, Leslie C. Mondesir, Damarys Scaff, mi prima Ivette Serrano, Lily Vento (Miss Yeye), Gwen Charles, Stephanie Amaro-Nieves, and France Tucker. Also, sincere thanks to Kelly Calabrese for early reads.

To the bestest friend/critique partner, Stephanie Jones. Our daily Facebook therapy sessions keep me sane! Let's keep grinding and popping out these stories.

To Sofia Quintero, Guadalupe Garcia McCall, and Carmen Bernier-Grand, gracias por leer y apoyar a mi libro. Attorney José A. Camacho of Camacho & Associates in Brooklyn, New York: thank you for helping me sort out the legal-speak for the news articles.

To Las Musas Marketing Collective, I adore the purpose and mission of our group. ¡Adelante!

To Darnell Davis and Deborah Smith-Gregory, thank you for the NAACP ACT-SO memories in high school. It was the time of my life!

I've always wanted a big sister. I'm happy to have found that in Karyn Parsons. Sending you so much love for your kindness and continued inspiration!

To Brian Edwards, part godfather, part long-lost uncle. Your advice and advocacy knows no limits.

To Debbie Allen, in whose honor this book is written. In hard times, girls like Beatriz Mendez seek out role models—whether real or intangible—to guide their path. Ms. Allen, your life's work is a legendary testament to every dancer and every dreamer across the globe.

And lastly, I thank you, the reader, for choosing this book. As I imagine you reading my words, I realize that there is no greater vision of a dream fulfilled.